DOG DAYS

Stories of My Four-Legged Friends

ROBERT PARKER

Published by Dolman Scott in 2024

Illustrations by Carol James (Carol@m-ybooks.co.uk)

ISBN:
PoD: 978-1-915351-25-8
eBook: 978-1-915351-26-5

Published by
DolmanScott
www.dolmanscott.com

TABLE OF CONTENTS

Robert Parker the author hard at work dreaming of new canine adventures

AN INTRODUCTION TO MAN'S BEST FRIEND

A dog is indeed an unparalleled companion for both men and women. Through my own experiences, I've found that dogs embody the epitome of loyalty, obedience, consistency, and unwavering faithfulness. They stand by our side through life's trials and triumphs, always eager to protect, comfort, and love unconditionally. Stories abound of dogs who, despite being separated from their humans, wait with unyielding hope for years on end for a joyful reunion. Tales of dogs braving the elements and overcoming obstacles to find their way back home only reaffirm the depth of their devotion. It raises the philosophical question of ownership—whether humans own dogs or if, perhaps, it's the dogs who possess our hearts. The optimal time to welcome a dog into your life is when they are between six to ten weeks old. Although separation from their mother at this tender age can be traumatic, it soon gives way to the formation of a profound bond with their new family. With time, love, and care, this bond solidifies into a lifelong, indestructible connection.

Throughout my lifetime, I have had the privilege of sharing my journey with eight remarkable dogs. Each one brought a unique set of traits that were utterly endearing, making every moment spent together a treasure. Sharing their discoveries of the natural world and cultivating an everlasting bond has been an immense joy. Although the sorrow at the end of their lives is profound, the memories we created are indelible.

This modest book is a tribute to those memories—a compilation of precious moments and experiences I had the fortune to share with my canine friends. It's an attempt to encapsulate the beauty and depth of the relationships formed with these extraordinary creatures.

For
Skip, Nutmeg, Wellington, Boots, Tigger, Millie, Jasper,
Alphie and Mungo.

WHO ARE YOU SKIP, AND WHY ARE YOU HERE?

The last rays of the afternoon sun were fading as I trudged off the bus from Bakewell, finding myself in the quaint embrace of Ashford in the Water. My thoughts were clouded with the disheartening reflections of my inaugural day at the new school. The journey home to The School House—a name that still felt foreign on my tongue despite having been my residence for a mere week—was short but filled with contemplation on what could have made the day bearable.

I mused over my father's simultaneous first day at his school, silently wishing his experiences had been more fulfilling than mine. As the familiar structures of the school and then our house came into view, curiosity nudged my disappointment aside. The priority was to ascertain how his day unfolded. But first, I reminded myself to adhere to the domestic discipline instilled by my mother: my blazer needed to find its way into the wardrobe, not abandoned in a heap on the floor or draped over my bed, lest I incur her displeasure.

The bedroom I had occupied for six nights had quickly endeared itself to me. Spacious and airy, it was a stark contrast to my previous abode, boasting a large picture window that offered a panoramic view of the River Wye and the rolling hills beyond. The prospect of exploring those hills, perhaps accompanied by a newfound friend, ignited a spark of excitement within me.

However, as I nudged the garden gate open, an unexpected sight halted me—a black and white ball of fluff, a burst of energy that momentarily appeared before skittering under the laurel bush at the garden's edge.

I froze, processing the sight. A dog?. No, a puppy, by the looks of it. Questions swirled in my mind about its origins and how it managed to infiltrate our garden, surrounded by formidable barriers meant to keep such intruders at bay.

The sudden sensation of a tap on my shoulder made me whirl around, coming face to face with my father, who excitedly pointed out the tiny intruder now making its cautious way across the lawn towards us. Despite my disbelief, I blurted out an offer to catch the apparently lost sheepdog puppy.

My father's response took me by surprise. "He's yours," he softly announced, "His name is Skip. Calling him should bring him to you."

Sure enough, within moments, Skip was in my arms, anointing my face with enthusiastic licks. The revelation that Skip was a gift for me, a symbol of a fresh start in this new chapter of our lives, left me speechless. My recent tumultuous history in Warsop, marked by mischief and admonishments, seemed a world away. Yet, here I was, being entrusted with a companion, a gesture of faith and love from my parents that felt like an unwarranted reward yet a profound opportunity for redemption.

Skip's arrival marked the beginning of a new bond, a shared journey of growth and healing, in the shadow of past troubles and towards a future filled with hope and companionship. It was a strange, beautiful twist in the narrative of my life, a testament to the unpredictable, gracious turns of fate.

SHEPHERDING THE SHEEP

The sudden urgency of the knocks on the door startled me from my academic reverie, the sharp raps demanding immediate attention. With a sigh, I set aside my fountain pen, carefully tucked my biology homework into the desk, and made my way through the hall toward the unexpected intrusion. My mother, however, with her innate responsiveness, had already reached the door, swinging it open to reveal the source of the commotion.

Standing there, with a storm brewing in his eyes, was George, the familiar farmer from Top Farm. His usually composed demeanor was nowhere to be seen, replaced instead by an aura of barely contained fury. With a knot of apprehension tightening my stomach, I pondered what could have possibly incited such wrath.

Before I could interject, George's thunderous voice filled the space, targeting our beloved Skip with a threat that sent chills down my spine. My mother's posture deflated under the weight of his words, a silent testament to her concern. I couldn't stand idly by. Stepping forward, I positioned myself between my mother and George, ready to bear the brunt of his anger. "He's my responsibility," I declared, the words heavy with a mixture of fear and defiance.

George paused, seemingly taken aback by my intervention. This moment of silence was merely the calm before the storm, as he launched into a detailed account of his ordeal. His narrative painted a vivid picture, The sprawling Harrup field, with its sea of green under the expansive sky, was a pastoral idyll and home to George's flock of ewes and their lambs. However, this tranquility was disrupted by the chaos unleashed by Skip.

It was a curious thing, George not having a dog, especially given the nature of his work. His absence of a canine companion on a farm teeming with livestock was a puzzle I had often contemplated but never solved.

As George's initial fury calmed down to a simmering frustration, he recounted the laborious task of selecting lambs for the market, a day's work rendered futile by Skip's unsanctioned herding escapade. The disappointment in his voice was palpable, especially as he mentioned Joyce's missed hair appointment—a casualty of their unexpected overtime in the field.

The final revelation of Skip's misadventure left me in a precarious position, torn between defending my loyal friend and facing the consequences of his actions. George's final query about Skip's whereabouts filled me with dread. Yet, as I stood there, a silent prayer on my lips, the quiet of the evening remained undisturbed, granting us a temporary reprieve from the storm of George's wrath.

In that moment, the depth of my bond with Skip became crystal clear—despite the chaos, the fear of loss, and the daunting responsibility his actions had thrust upon me, I knew that navigating these turbulent waters was part of the journey of companionship and love that we shared.

"WHO THE HELL ARE YOU?"

The urgency in my mother's voice sliced through the afternoon calm, her words laden with concern for Skip, our adventurous Collie who seemed to have embarked on an unsanctioned exploration of the village. The realisation that Skip was missing from his usual haunts in our backyard sent a ripple of anxiety through me. "How long has he been gone?" I shouted towards the kitchen, secretly hoping for reassurance that his disappearance was a recent event. The mixer's whir humming in the background only heightened the tension. My mother confessed she had no idea of his whereabouts, her focus divided between baking and the crisis.

Resigned to my role in the rescue mission and reminded of the non-negotiable nature of maternal directives, I donned my jacket with a mix of haste and reluctance. The Hall Orchard, a communal treasure and the village's verdant heart, seemed the most plausible destination for a dog with Skip's curious inclinations.

Upon arrival, my query to a group of children, engrossed in their playground antics, was met with a disdainful disregard, a stark reminder of my less-than-favourable reputation among the younger village residents. Their blunt refusal to aid in my search only fueled my frustration, prompting me to widen my search toward the cricket field.

The cricket field presented a bittersweet tableau; friends immersed in their game, a scene I longed to join but duty bound me elsewhere. Alan's cricket prowess momentarily distracted me, a testament to the camaraderie I was missing. Yet, the urgency to find Skip tugged at me, pulling me away from the fleeting joy of the game.

The failing light and the growl of hunger pangs hinted at the day's end, compelling me to consider admitting defeat. The thought of returning home empty-handed was disheartening, yet the promise of a hearty supper offered some small consolation.

However, fate had a twist in store. As I neared the village's heart, a familiar black and white figure emerged, igniting a flicker of hope. "Skip!" I called, desperation lacing my voice, only to be met with a response that was anything but reassuring. Skip's evasion seemed a stark denial of our bond, his distance growing with every call I made.

The chase that ensued was a test of wills, winding through the village's arteries, a silent plea for recognition hanging between us. The sight of Skip veering into our home's embrace offered a glimmer of hope, a potential end to this unexpected odyssey.

There, before the threshold of our home, sat Skip, the embodiment of innocent mischief, his wagging tail and direct gaze seemingly asking, "You wanted me home, didn't you?" His presence, both a relief and a rebuke, was a reminder of the unspoken pact between us—a bond of trust, companionship, and the occasional chase. In that moment, all frustrations melted away, replaced by the warmth of reunion and the silent acknowledgment of the adventures and misadventures that lay in the heart of our shared journey.

HE'S GONE BACK TO UNI.
I HAD BETTER GO AND FIND HIM

The persistent rain drummed a rhythmic pattern against the windows, a soundtrack to Greta's firm instruction that Bob should venture into the storm in search of their wayward Collie, Skip. Bob, though swamped with the daunting task of preparing school lessons, couldn't ignore the directive. He donned his mac, a protective shield against the downpour, his mind swirling with thoughts of Skip's unusual escapade. It was out of character for Skip to stray, making his absence more perplexing.

The quest to find Skip turned into an exhaustive search, spanning every conceivable locale from the farm at the lane's end to the village's communal heartbeat, and even the local pubs, places brimming with familiar faces yet devoid of any sign of Skip. Upon his return, soaked and disheartened, Bob found solace in Greta's pragmatic optimism. Supper awaited, albeit slightly overdone, a small comfort against the backdrop of worry for their absent friend.

The new day dawned with no sign of Skip, escalating their concern into action. Greta's call to the local police yielded no immediate hope, leaving them to grapple with the silence of uncertainty. However, the unexpected call from Bakewell police station later that day sparked a flicker of hope. The detailed description of a found Collie in Matlock, a good distance away, matched Skip's appearance and behaviors uncannily. Bob couldn't help but smile at the image of Skip, detained yet untroubled, in a police cell.

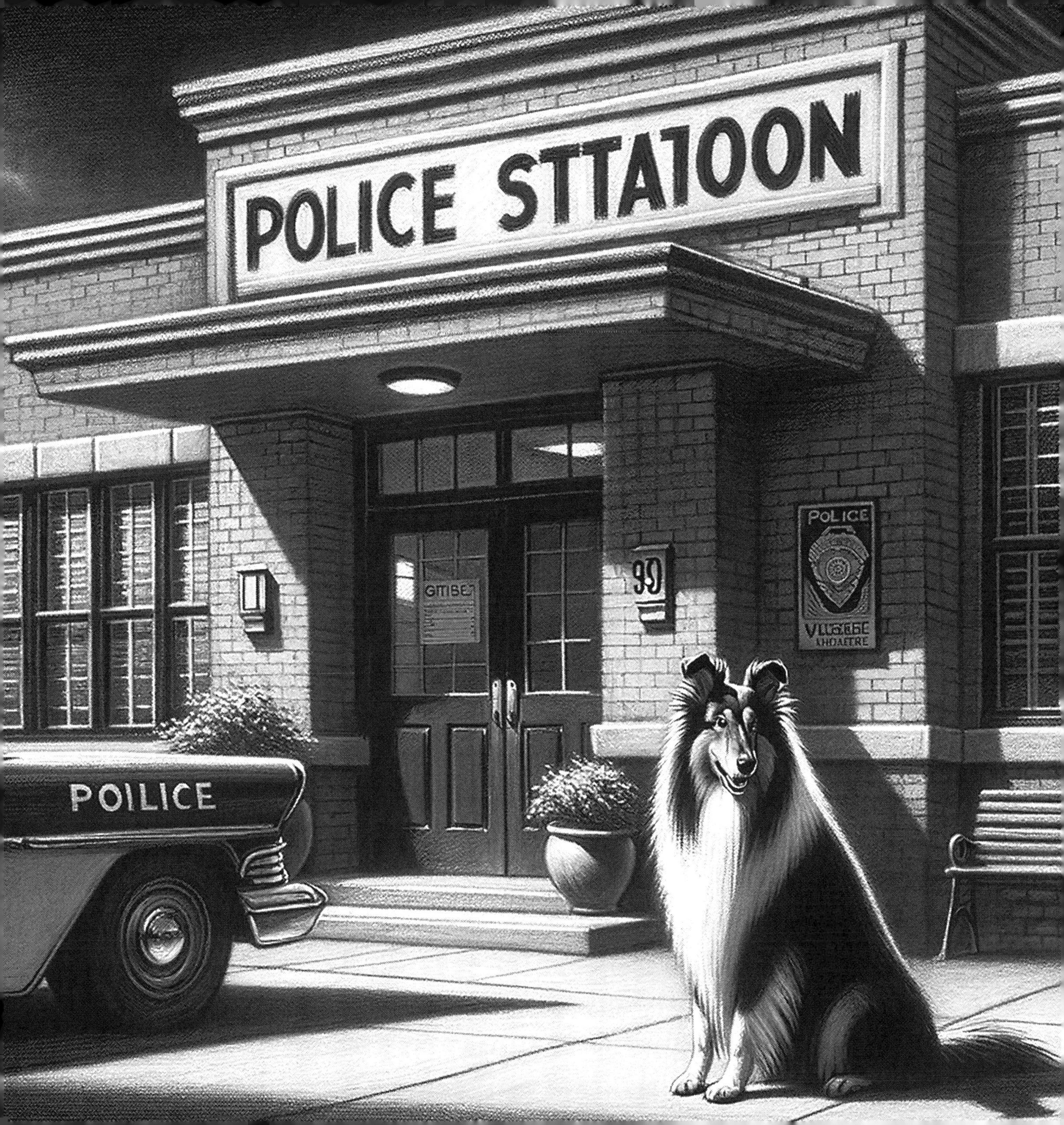
POLICE STTATOON
POLICE
POILICE

The revelation that Skip might have embarked on a quest to find their son, Robert, who had recently returned to university, painted his journey in a new light. The lengths to which Skip had gone, driven by loyalty and perhaps a sense of loss, astounded them. Matlock, with its distance and dangers, seemed an improbable destination for any dog, yet Skip had defied the odds.

Greta's conversation with the Matlock police further confirmed their hopes. The description matched Skip perfectly, right down to the distinctive black tail with its white tip. Their journey to Matlock, filled with anxious anticipation, culminated in a reunion that was both immediate and emotional. Skip's demeanor, unphased by his adventure, mirrored the simplicity of a dog's world where such escapades are mere blips in the continuum of their loyalty and love.

Home again, with Skip contentedly enjoying his supper, the ordeal seemed to dissolve into the fabric of family lore. For Skip, the adventure was just another day in his life, a testament to the boundless spirit and enduring bond that pets share with their families.

NUTMEG ARRIVES AT RECTORY.

The thrill of welcoming Nutmeg, the Irish Setter, into our home was palpable. Her previous visits had painted her as nothing short of delightful—a vision of elegance with her curly, nutmeg-brown fur and a demeanor that radiated charm. Yet, the abrupt departure of Sandra, her previous owner, with a finality that spoke volumes, should have been our first clue to the impending whirlwind Nutmeg was about to unleash upon our serene Rectory life.

Our evening out with friends was a brief respite from the anticipation of integrating Nutmeg into our family. The night was serene, with the celestial tapestry overhead whispering the calm before the storm. However, upon our return, the silence that greeted us was not the peaceful quietude we had expected but the ominous prelude to chaos unfurled.

The sight that met our eyes upon opening the drawing room door was one of bewildering astonishment. A scene reminiscent of a midwinter snowstorm unfolded before us, with what appeared to be countless snowflakes blanketing every surface. The realisation that these "snowflakes" were in fact the remains of what once were our plush, floral curtains—meticulously dismantled by Nutmeg in our absence—sent a shockwave of disbelief through us. Nutmeg's nose, barely visible behind the sofa, and her sheepish, almost contrite expression did little to temper the magnitude of her misadventure.

In one evening, Nutmeg had transformed from a seemingly gentle soul into a whirlwind of destruction, leaving us to ponder the true nature of her spiritedness. Her artistic endeavor, while destructive, was a stark reminder of the unpredictability that comes with opening one's home

to a new pet. The missing curtains, now transformed into a landscape of faux snow, stood as a testament to Nutmeg's untapped energy and perhaps a mischievous streak that Sandra had alluded to, albeit subtly.

As we stood amidst the aftermath, the weight of Nutmeg's "handiwork" settled upon us, not just as a loss of material possessions but as an unforeseen challenge that lay ahead. It was a vivid introduction to the complexities and joys of pet ownership, a journey that, while sometimes fraught with unexpected turns, promised to enrich our lives with unconditional love, laughter, and the occasional reminder of the sheer unpredictability of sharing one's life with a spirited canine.

NUTMEG AND THE FOX

The tale of Nutmeg and the vixen is one that transcends the ordinary encounters between domestic pets and wild animals, weaving a narrative of unexpected camaraderie against the backdrop of Yate Hall's neglected splendor. The mansion's serene desolation, alongside the untamed beauty of its fox residents, set the stage for a remarkable interaction that speaks volumes about the instincts and intelligence of animals.

Nutmeg, despite her previous rambunctious behavior within the confines of the Rectory, showcased a different facet of her nature during the twilight encounter with the vixen. Her poised observation, followed by a silent release to chase, not hunt, reveals a complex understanding and restraint uncharacteristic of many domesticated dogs when confronted with wildlife.

The chase, rather than culminating in a violent clash as one might fear, unfolded as a breathtaking dance across the Rectory's fields. It was a chase devoid of malice, where the thrill of the run united predator and playmate in a moment of pure freedom. Nutmeg's ability to match the vixen stride for stride, yet choose companionship over conquest, showcases a rare moment of interspecies understanding and respect.

This momentary bond, fleeting as it was, left an indelible mark on Nutmeg, whose subsequent searches along the wall seemed driven by a hope for another playful rendezvous rather than a predatory impulse. It's a poignant reminder of the potential for harmony in the natural world, even between the most unlikely of friends.

The legacy of that evening's encounter goes beyond the thrill of the chase; it's a testament to the unexpected connections that can occur between the worlds of the wild and the tamed. Nutmeg's story, set against the backdrop of Yate Hall's quiet grandeur, adds a layer of mystique and wonder to the life within and around the Rectory, encapsulating the beauty of nature's unpredictability and the endless possibilities that lie in the simple act of crossing paths.

WELLINGTON EATING THE CHICKENS AND EGGS

From the moment I heard about Wellington, a lively puppy born on a farm in the picturesque mid-Wales, I knew my life was about to change. He was the only male in a litter of six, and by the time I arrived to pick, it was Wellington or no one. It wasn't much of a choice, but as fate would have it, he was the perfect choice for me.

Three months later, Wellington wasn't just a pet; he was my shadow, my constant companion. We were inseparable, sharing a bond that seemed to deepen with every passing day. But then, a challenge loomed on the horizon. I had plans to visit my parents, who had recently moved to a quaint seaside village in Lincolnshire, 200 miles away. They were living their dream retirement by the sea, a dream that inconveniently placed them quite a distance from me.

The thought of leaving Wellington behind for the weekend was unbearable. My parents knew I had a dog, but the logistics of bringing him along hadn't been discussed. So, I decided to call them, bracing myself for a difficult conversation. To my surprise, my mother cut me short, insisting Wellington come along. She drew a heartwarming parallel between Wellington and Skip, the Collie we had when I was younger. The problem was solved before it truly became one.

The next morning, Wellington and I set off early, him comfortably nestled in the back of the estate car, separated by a dog guard but content. The journey was smooth, Wellington snoozing for the most part, except for a brief stop for a leg stretch.

Arriving at my parents', Wellington was greeted with as much love and enthusiasm as any family member. Their excitement at meeting him was matched only by Wellington's joy at discovering the beach. He frolicked in the surf, chased balls, and simply reveled in the new experiences, making me see the world anew through his eyes.

That evening, after a delicious dinner prepared by my mother, we settled down for a game of bridge with Mabel, a neighbor. Despite my dad and I being soundly defeated, the evening was filled with laughter and warmth.

Sunday morning brought a light breakfast and preparations for church. With my dad leading the service, we decided to leave Wellington in the conservatory, thinking it the safest option. Little did we know, Wellington had other plans. Returning home, we were greeted by a scene of culinary devastation. Wellington had managed to eat an entire chicken meant for lunch, along with two and a half dozen eggs. My mother's distress was palpable, her pitch almost beyond my comprehension as she lamented the loss.

In the end, we opted for lunch at the pub, my treat, marking an end to a weekend that was anything but ordinary. Wellington, under the worktop with just his anxious eyes showing, seemed to understand the chaos he'd caused. Yet, as we drove home, I couldn't help but smile at the memories we'd made. Wellington, in his own mischievous way, had brought us closer, turning an ordinary visit into an unforgettable adventure.

WELLINGTON FALLING INTO THE RIVER

I'll never forget the day I discovered Wellington's secret. He was more than just a beloved companion; he was a beacon of joy for the residents of the nursing home where we spent our days. Wellington, alongside his friend Bubbles—or Boots, as we affectionately called the Tibetan Spaniel—had a routine of visiting everyone, offering comfort and companionship that seemed to lighten the weight of the world.

Our regular walks by the River Severn were the highlight of our days. The vast meadows and the tranquil river, prone to its dramatic floods, provided a perfect backdrop for our adventures. It was on one of these walks, on a warm day in May, amidst the vibrant colors of spring, that Wellington's true condition came to light.

As we strolled along the riverbank, flanked by hawthorn bushes blooming with May flowers, a moment of confusion led to a heart-stopping incident. Wellington, usually so sure-footed, seemed to vanish into thin air, only to reappear with a splash in the river below. His subsequent actions, swimming in seemingly random directions, filled me with dread and confusion. It was a puzzle, each of his choices more baffling than the last, until the terrifying truth dawned on us—Wellington couldn't see. He was blind.

The realisation hit like a thunderbolt. How had we not noticed? How had he navigated his world in darkness with such confidence and joy? A visit to the vet, followed by a specialist's confirmation, revealed the irreversible damage to his optic nerve. Yet, this discovery didn't

dampen his spirits. Wellington continued to live his life with the same zest and enthusiasm he always had, undeterred by his blindness.

He lived a full life, reaching the grand age of eighteen and a half years. His affinity for water never waned; he would plunge into it with the same eagerness, each time as if it were a new discovery. Wellington's story taught me about resilience, the ability to find joy and purpose despite the challenges. He was more than just a dog; he was a lesson in courage, a testament to the strength of spirit over the limitations of the body. Wellington may have been blind, but he saw the world in a way that I could only aspire to—a world filled with love, trust, and the sheer joy of being alive.

BUBBLES IN THE TUNNEL

Waking up to a world transformed overnight into a winter wonderland was a moment of pure magic. The snow lay thick and untouched, a blanket of silence covering everything in sight. With excitement bubbling inside me, I couldn't wait to step out into this fresh canvas of snow. Donning my wellies, I called for Wellington and Bubbles, eager to introduce them to their first snowfall.

Boots, or Bubbles as he's fondly known, is a spirited little Tibetan Spaniel with an indomitable will. Despite his small stature, he possesses a heart as fierce as any lion's, never backing down, no matter the size of his opponent. Wellie, on the other hand, approached the snow with a palpable sense of trepidation. His blindness, usually a mere footnote to his adventurous spirit, seemed to cast a longer shadow in the unfamiliar snowy landscape. The snow muffled the world around us, making it harder for him to navigate by scent.

Bubbles, contrastingly, was a whirlwind of energy, darting about in sheer delight. He dove into snowdrifts with abandon, each leap a testament to his joyous discovery of the snow's playful potential.

After our initial foray into the snowy garden, we retreated indoors, warmed by thoughts of breakfast and the adventures yet to come. I resolved that after church, we would undertake the quintessential winter activity: building a snowman. I imagined it would be a perfect way to spend the afternoon, especially if the village children joined in the fun.

True to plan, as the morning service concluded and the last drops of coffee were savored, we ventured back outside. To my delight, Sophie and Shaun from the nearby farm had come over, eager to assist in our snowman construction. Their presence promised an afternoon filled with laughter and communal joy.

However, as we set about our task, Bubbles disappeared, sending a ripple of panic through me. The mischievous grins on Sophie and Shaun's faces, however, hinted at a playful conspiracy. And sure enough, Bubbles wasn't lost but rather playfully buried in the snow, a hidden treasure waiting to burst forth.

His emergence from his snowy cocoon was like a rebirth, a spectacle met with laughter and cheers. It was a moment of pure, unadulterated joy, reminding me of the simple pleasures life offers.

That day, as we stood back to admire our handiwork—a snowman standing guard in the garden, with Wellington cautiously sniffing around its base and Bubbles prancing about, reinvigorated from his brief 'burial'—I felt a profound sense of gratitude. Despite Wellington's challenges and Bubbles' impish tendencies, or perhaps because of them, they brought endless warmth and light into my life, proving that love and joy can indeed flourish, even in the coldest of winters.

WELLINGTON MEETS TIGGER.

Gina burst into my life like a comet, illuminating everything with her presence and leaving me to marvel at the sudden change in my trajectory. She lived near Taunton, a distance that seemed trivial compared to the connection we shared. Our meetings, though few, hinted at a future filled with possibilities, a future we both eagerly anticipated.

However, life, with its impeccable timing, presented a challenge. My impending trip to the USA to visit my daughter and her husband in Silicon Valley meant I had to find care for Wellington, my blind Collie. The thought of leaving him in kennels, given his condition, was unbearable.

Gina's offer to take Wellington into her home in Taunton was a lifeline. "Bring him down to Taunton," she had said effortlessly during one of our evening calls. Her confidence and willingness to help eased my concern. She assured me that Wellington and her boxer, Tigger, would coexist peacefully during my absence.

The journey to Gina's, the old vicarage at Angersleigh, was filled with a mix of anticipation and anxiety. Upon arrival, Gina and an exuberant Tigger greeted me. The energy was infectious, but a sense of apprehension lingered as the time came to introduce Wellington to his temporary companion.

The moment Wellington leapt from the car, Tigger, in true boxer fashion, greeted him with an enthusiastic bounce, a gesture that ended in an unexpected collision. Wellington, taken by surprise and unable to see the assault coming, reacted defensively. The situation escalated

quickly into a flurry of barks and growls, a chaotic introduction that marked the beginning of their wary relationship.

Over time, their initial wariness evolved into a cautious acceptance, and eventually, into a companionship characterized by peaceful coexistence. The transformation was gradual, their shared moments in front of the Aga becoming a testament to their reconciliation. As they aged, they found comfort in each other's presence, lying nose to nose, embodying an unlikely friendship born out of necessity and nurtured by patience and understanding.

Their relationship was a reminder that bonds can form in the most unexpected circumstances, growing stronger through trials and time. Wellington and Tigger, with their contrasting personalities and challenges, taught me that even the most unlikely friendships can flourish, offering warmth, companionship, and a sense of belonging. In their golden years, as they dozed in harmony by the warmth of the Aga, they were a living symbol of reconciliation and the power of mutual acceptance.

MILLIE AND JASPER COME TO TEDSMORE

We parked the car next to the hen house and walked the twenty yards to the farmhouse door. I knocked tentatively. After what seemed an absolute age, the door swung open and we were confronted by an enormous woman, wearing a tweed skirt, and a very low-cut blouse. She must have been in her sixties but was clearly trying to give the impression of being a woman who was somewhat younger. "You have some Labrador puppies for sale", I ventured. "We rang about them an hour ago, and you said that we could come and see them"

Without a word, the woman turned and led us inside. In the kitchen we met her son. "Come through", he said, and led us on into the sitting room. It was sparsely furnished, and clearly the furniture had in the most part seen better days.

"'They are over there", he said, motioning towards a large box in the corner. "There are four left, 3 black boys, and a chocolate girl, but she's not for sale, mum has decided that she wants to keep her.'

We moved closer to the large box, and the chocolate puppy stood up wagging her tail.

Then the largest of the black boys decided to jump out of the box and come and greet us. Suddenly the chocolate puppy also leapt out from the box and rushed over to us wagging her tail. I picked her up, and she affectionately licked my face. I put her down, and she tried to leap back into my arms! She repeated the same movement several times. Gina was still holding the little black boy. "Can we have him", she whispered, "he's adorable".

"He's lovely", I said, as I rapidly agreed, and then I turned to the young farmer and said "Can we have both the black boy, and the chocolate girl?"

What we didn't know until that moment was that they already had names   Their mother was called Gloria and the two pups that we were keen to acquire were Albert and Doris. But, of course, that was soon to be changed.

He sidled over to the woman (who turned out to be his mother) and they spent what seemed an age whispering about 'Albert and Doris', and then 'My mum was going to keep Doris, but for £1,000 they are yours'

They had an instant change of name and Jasper and Millie came home with us ten minutes later.

GETTING UNDER THE SOFA
IN THE TV ROOM

"Getting Under the Sofa" is a charming tale that captures the mischief and learning curve of raising puppies. Below is a refined and expanded version of your story, aimed at enhancing detail, narrative flow, and emotional depth:

~

Getting Under the Sofa

In the family TV room, chaos is often just a puppy's whim away. Raising two puppies simultaneously—Millie, a chocolate lab, and Jasper, a black spaniel—is a venture overflowing with joy and mischief. Their thick, glossy coats and boundless energy fill our days with light, even though managing their antics is a full-time job.

At twelve weeks old, Millie and Jasper are surprisingly quick learners. Commands like 'Come here', 'Sit', 'Stay', and 'Bring it to me' are met with increasing reliability, although Jasper often glances at his sister, as if seeking approval, before deciding whether to heed my calls. Their world so far has been somewhat limited, encompassing their cosy dog room, the bustling kitchen, and the expansive freedom of the garden.

Yesterday, I decided it was time to broaden their horizons. We took our first full tour around the cross-country course—a good mile and a half of varied terrain. They handled it admirably,

their noses twitching eagerly at each new scent and hidden thicket along the way. Buoyed by this success, I resolved to further their exploration to the interiors of the house. Starting tonight, the TV room would be their new frontier.

As evening settled, the pups joined us on the plush leather sofa, curling up into slumbering balls after a hearty meal. The choice of a wildlife documentary about African reptiles seemed a perfect backdrop to a peaceful night. However, the frequent commercial breaks gave the tranquility a staccato feel. During one such interruption, Gina and I stepped out—she to fetch a cardigan against the evening chill, and I to top up our glasses with a vibrant New Zealand Sauvignon Blanc, its lemony zest a perfect palate cleanser.

Upon our return, the scene before us halted our steps. Gina, pale as a ghost at the threshold, mirrored my shock. Feathers everywhere. What had been a pristine room was now a snowstorm of down. The culprits? Millie and Jasper embroiled in what could only be described as a full-blown pillow fight. The remains of a once-sturdy cushion lay between them, gutted completely.

"Millie! Stop!" My voice thundered through the chaos, followed swiftly by, "Jasper, no!" At my command, both puppies ceased their feathered frenzy and darted for the safety of the sofa, squeezing into their favorite hideout beneath it. Only their guilty eyes peered out, clearly stating they had no intention of coming closer.

"Come here," I tried again, modulating my tone to a mix of firmness and coaxing. Silence. It took ten minutes of gentle persuasion before they tentatively approached, their demeanor sheepish.

Despite my initial frustration, anger melted into forgiveness as they sidled up to me. They seemed to understand the gravity of their mischief—under the sofa was their sanctuary, but not an excuse for unruliness.

Over the next six months, "under the sofa" became their go-to haven for any perceived threat, though it was never again used as a refuge post-cushion assault. We'd learned our lesson and relocated all cushions to the safety of the drawing rooms.

Time passed, and the puppies grew. One evening, as Gina and I prepared dessert, another episode of chaos unfolded. This time, a newspaper bore the brunt of their playful aggression, ending up in tatters across the floor. As we re-entered, the sight of their devastation prompted another instinctive retreat. They dashed for the sofa, but their increased size thwarted their escape. Struggling in vain, they finally gave up and turned to face us, eyes downcast, ready to confront the consequences of their actions.

"Getting Under the Sofa" in the TV room had transformed from a literal hiding spot into a metaphor for growing up—realizing some mistakes are too big to hide from, no matter how hard you try.

THE YOUNG DEER

August painted the landscape in strokes of vibrant green and gold. It was the peak of summer, and the river Coquet dazzled under the sun's affectionate gaze, its waters a tapestry of shimmering light.

Jasper, now eighteen months old, reveled in the coolness of the river, fetching sticks with youthful zeal. His twin, Millie, approached the water's edge with her usual elegance—paddling gently rather than plunging in. Her demeanor seemed to say, "Fetch? Me? Surely you jest. I am far too dignified for such frivolity."

We were tracing the well-worn path home, sandwiched between the undulating cornfield and the tranquil river, with thoughts of a warm cup of coffee awaiting us. But serenity gave way to sudden excitement when, about fifty yards ahead, two heads popped up from the amber waves of grain.

A pair of roe deer—a hind and her fawn—had been startled by our presence. Millie and Jasper, instincts triggered, surged forward like bolts from a bow. The deer, in a desperate bid for safety, darted through the cornfield. The fawn, not as swift as its mother, lagged dangerously behind.

"Millie, no—come here!" I called, my voice thundering futilely across the distance.

It was too late. Millie, her retriever instincts in full display, closed the gap swiftly and brought the young deer down. From a distance, the mother deer turned, watching helplessly.

My heart sank as Millie, triumphant, trotted back through the swaying corn with the lifeless fawn. She laid her grim trophy at my feet, tail wagging, eyes sparkling with pride. "Look, Dad, I've done well, haven't I? This is what I am—a retriever!"

The gravity of the moment struck me hard. Despite the raw display of instinctual behavior, scolding her would serve no purpose. She had merely acted according to her nature.

With heavy hearts, we withdrew, leaving the fallen fawn by the riverside, a somber offering for the mother to reclaim. It was a stark reminder of the wildness that underlies even our most beloved companions' playful antics—a lesson in the brutal realities of nature, witnessed on a golden August day.

STALKING THE RABBIT

Boxing Day brought a crisp -6°C chill that clung to the air, the remnants of a week-long freeze. A light snowfall had dusted the landscape, solidifying the ground beneath a thin, crunchy veil. It was an idyllic scene for a walk—sky a stark blue, air still, serene.

Our lunch had been modest, the leftovers from Christmas providing a feast for the Labs—Millie and Jasper. Skins and gristle from the turkey and a sausage or two had them ready for what they cherished most: a walk. At the mention, they were instantly at my side, tails wagging, eyes alight with the promise of adventure.

Bundled up—myself in hat, coat, and gloves (not the Labs!)—we set off towards the cross-country course. This loop, about a mile and a half of mixed woodland and open pasture, was their daily playground, a place rich with the scents and trails of rabbits, squirrels, badgers, and other woodland denizens. Here, they roamed free, untethered and full of vigor.

Midway through our walk, as we approached a dense copse by the local reservoir, the dogs suddenly surged ahead. A thicket of yew, bracken, and bramble was their target, and the cause of their excitement quickly became clear. Three buzzards, previously grounded near the thicket, erupted into flight, startled by the Labs' enthusiastic charge.

I caught up to find Millie and Jasper circling the thicket, noses down, tails high. They were on the trail of a large rabbit, which had sought refuge there, presumably from the buzzards now

circling overhead. Despite their eagerness, the dense cover thwarted their every attempt to reach the frightened animal. After a few minutes, I called them off, realizing the futility of their efforts.

The scene left me puzzled. Buzzards, I knew, typically hunted from the skies, not the ground. It seemed they had adapted, cornering their prey where it thought itself safe. "No chance that rabbit will become their meal," I thought, observing the ample hiding spots within the thicket.

However, a return trip to the area just after sunset painted a grim update. Near the thicket, on the icy ground, lay the rabbit—lifeless, disemboweled, its brain consumed. The buzzards, it appeared, were not just adept at aerial hunting but had mastered the art of ground ambush as well.

This encounter left me pondering the adaptability of nature's hunters and the stark realities of the food chain. Even in the serene backdrop of a winter's walk, life and death danced closely, intertwined in the survival instincts of the animal kingdom.

CHASING THE HARE.

The day was brisk and filled with the promise of adventure as we arrived in Northumberland, the first trip to this storied landscape for the two Labrador pups, now ten months old. No sooner had the car been emptied than I was mounting the quad bike—dogs eagerly bounding beside me—and heading for the river.

The Coquet, a clear, gurgling river that weaves its way through the lush countryside to meet the sea near Warkworth Castle, was particularly delightful that day. We crossed the Guyzance Estate, our path cutting through the stubble of a recently harvested wheat field. It was here that a hare, hidden until that moment in its shallow scoop, burst forth just yards from the unsuspecting labs.

With the hare in sudden flight, Millie and Jasper leaped into action, their bodies a blur of chocolate and black fur. The chase was fervent but brief; within thirty yards, it was clear the hare was outmatching them, its swift, agile bounds putting it quickly out of reach. After a hundred yards, the pups, conceding defeat, trotted back to me, sides heaving.

At the river, both dogs indulged in their favorite pastime—fetching sticks thrown into the mid-river, then laying them at my feet for another go. The water was invigorating, and they swam several times, their spirits undampened by the earlier chase.

As the sun began its descent, signaling our time to head home, we navigated through a pasture dotted with thistles and patches of nettles. It was then another hare made its daring escape from

a shallow dip in the field. Jasper, ever the optimist, charged with gusto. The hare, swift and sure, was halfway across the meadow in mere seconds, Jasper's ambitious efforts futile from the start.

Turning to Millie, I noticed she hadn't budged. She stood by my side, head tilted, eyes shining with a mix of amusement and exasperation. It was as if she was thinking, "You silly boy, Jasper. We just tried this. You know we can't catch them. Come back, let's head home for supper."

Her look said it all: a blend of wisdom and sibling tease, knowing well the limits of their abilities against the fleet-footed wild hares. Jasper's chase was a lesson in futility, one he seemed destined to repeat until he learned, as Millie had, the art of choosing his battles.

As Jasper finally slowed, acknowledging the inevitable, we resumed our journey home. The day's adventures had taught them both something about their capabilities and the nature of their world—lessons sure to be remembered on many walks to come.

THE TRAIN FROM HELSBY

The telephone's abrupt ring shattered the morning calm. "Mr. Parker, we have a problem at the hotel. The swimming pool pump has failed, and replacing it will cost at least $17,000, possibly more."

I sighed, rubbing my temples. "I'd better come and see it myself and talk with the engineers."

By next morning, I was up by 6:00, ready to tackle the logistics of getting to Edinburgh from our little hamlet. The plan was straightforward: a twenty-mile drive to Helsby to catch the train, with just one change at Warrington. However, a complication loomed—my wife was away, leaving me solely responsible for Millie and Jasper, our two Labrador twins. Not wanting to leave them behind, I decided they would accompany me on their first train journey ever. A challenge indeed, considering they had never even worn leashes, thanks to our spacious, rural living conditions.

We reached the station with time to spare. After ensuring my briefcase and a warm jacket were in order, I readied the leashes. "No, Millie, stay Jasper," I muttered as I opened the car door. Within moments, though, they were leashed and we were embarking on what I hoped wouldn't be too chaotic of an endeavor.

The walk to the platform was short. We turned right to face the footbridge that led to the platform for the train from Chester. That's when the leashes went taut. I turned to see both dogs sitting on their haunches, hackles raised, eyes locked on the bridge. It was an old-style structure with open treads—you could see straight through to the tracks below.

"Dad, that looks very dangerous," their wary eyes seemed to say. "You can see through it; we're not going up there."

"Come on, Millie, come on, Jasper," I coaxed, giving the leashes a gentle tug. The resistance was palpable—they hadn't budged. I tried again with a firmer tone, "Come on. NOW." Still, they remained unmoved, their bodies tensed against the unknown.

Then, as if reaching an unspoken agreement, they relaxed. Their bodies loosened and, within twenty seconds, we were over the bridge and onto the platform.

Victory!

As we settled to wait for the train, I couldn't help but smile at their brave faces, now looking around with a mixture of curiosity and pride. This journey, I realized, was more than just a trip to resolve a hotel issue—it was a leap into the unknown for Millie and Jasper, a test of their trust in me, and perhaps a small adventure that spoke to their hearts as much as it did to mine.

BACON SANDWICHES
COURTESY OF VIRGIN TRAINS

Warrington Bank Quay station was bustling as always. With trains to London departing several times an hour and connections to cities like Edinburgh, Glasgow, Manchester, and Liverpool, it was a hub of ceaseless activity. Freight and parcel trains added to the mix, making the station a rail enthusiast's paradise.

It was a cold, frosty Tuesday morning. The clear blue skies were intermittently crisscrossed by aircraft descending toward Manchester airport. The 7:22 AM train to London was delayed—again—causing a buildup of frustrated passengers on platform 3. Meanwhile, a freight train thundered on the down main, and a Liverpool commuter train eased into platform 4 with barely a whisper.

Amid this orchestrated chaos, I stood in Zone J, leashes in hand, with Millie and Jasper at my side. Having managed the initial challenge at Helsby and the unexpected bridge crossing, the Labs had adapted surprisingly well. They'd even tackled the short hop to Warrington aboard a Manchester train without incident. Now, we awaited the 7:27 AM train to Edinburgh, which was running ten minutes late. Fifteen minutes to go, and the dogs were calm, sitting patiently despite the hubbub.

Suddenly, a flurry of activity stirred the crowd as the Edinburgh train appeared in the distance. A woman in a red coat, her oversized feathered hat making her unmistakable, realized she and her teenagers were waiting in the wrong spot. She bellowed at them to move to where the standard carriages would stop.

The train eased to a halt, and the door to coach J slid open right in front of us. I boarded first, relieved to find that Millie and Jasper followed me onto the train like seasoned travelers. Inside, the coach was nearly empty. I stowed my briefcase, took a seat by a table, and the dogs settled next to me, as if this was a routine part of their day.

No sooner had we started moving than the train manager appeared, stopping mid-sentence upon noticing the dogs. "Sir, let me get them some water," he said, before I could even show my tickets. Moments later, he returned with two dog bowls labeled "Virgin Dog" and bottles of still water. After filling the bowls and handing me the bottles, he disappeared without checking my tickets.

Within a minute, another staff member appeared. "Sir, would you like some breakfast?" she asked, then noticing the Labs, added, "What are their names?" After introductions, she offered not only a full English breakfast for me but also bacon sandwiches for Millie and Jasper. Before I could even respond, she was off to prepare the order.

As we approached Wigan, the waitress returned with a steaming plate for me and bacon-loaded sandwiches for the dogs. She carefully placed the plates on the table, beaming. "Breakfast for the dogs, sir. I do hope they enjoy it."

Millie and Jasper wasted no time diving into their unexpected treat. The untouched water bowls stood in stark contrast to the swiftly devoured bacon sandwiches.

Their contented faces made it clear: train travel could become a regular part of their lives—as long as it was aboard a Virgin train, preferably in first class!

THE SQUIRREL AND THE THREE BLEEDING NOSES

The eternal animosity between Labradors and squirrels at Tedsmore had become a sort of legend. Millie, Jasper, and Digger, all from the same litter and makeshift triplets, had been giving the local squirrels a tough time since their puppy days. Not that they had ever caught one—squirrels are wily creatures—but the chases were frequent and fervent, filled with many near misses.

On this glorious May morning, as the estate was bursting with blossom, it seemed the squirrels were out in force, perhaps gathering food for their young. The Labs and I were walking through Home Wood, past the cross-country track by the lambing fields, and on to Reservoir Wood. Squirrels darted everywhere: up trees, across fields unusually far from any trees, perhaps searching for something other than nuts.

As we neared the homeward stretch, with breakfast for the Labs and a well-earned coffee for me just ten minutes away, another grey "tree rat" appeared by a shrub off the path. It was curiously oblivious to the presence of the Labs—or so it seemed. But Digger noticed, and in a flash, he was off, barreling towards the squirrel with a speed I hadn't seen him muster in a chase before.

"Digger, come back here! Leave it alone!" I shouted. Too late. He had the squirrel by the scruff, but almost immediately, a scream—not from the squirrel, but from Digger. The squirrel, while injured, was not defeated; it bared its teeth, and in a fierce counterattack, bit Digger on the nose. Blood streamed down as he circled in pain, the squirrel half-lying on the ground, still defiant.

No sooner had Digger retreated than Jasper decided to join the fray, undeterred by the sight of his brother's injury. "Jasper, no—come here!" My command fell on deaf ears. He lunged for the squirrel's neck and was promptly rewarded with his own sharp nip to the nose, yelping as he joined Digger in painful circles.

Now, Millie, seeing her brothers' plight, lunged forward. I doubted calling her off would do any good—and I was right. She too underestimated the small but fierce adversary and soon was running in circles with a bloodied nose, just like the others.

The squirrel, though clearly injured, was a fighter. It lay on the ground, panting and hurt, but its spirit unbroken, ready to defend itself against any further attacks.

As we walked home, the Labs, each with a bloodied nose, seemed to have learned a valuable lesson. While their pursuit of squirrels didn't end that day, they adopted a more cautious approach in future encounters, always keeping just out of reach.

This surprising turn of events led me to muse on the unexpected intelligence and adaptability of dogs. Perhaps there is wisdom even in their mistakes, a lesson in the limits of bravery and the wisdom of caution.

I SHALL WATCH YOU IN CHURCH

This morning, with Gina away in Devon and me tasked with leading the service at St. Peter's Church in Sutton Coldfield, I found myself in a bit of a predicament. Responsible for our three Labradors—Millie, Mungo, and Alphie—I decided they would accompany me to church for the first time. They were well-behaved dogs, but I packed leashes just in case.

After loading my robes and sermon notes into the car, I called the dogs. "Now, come on Millie, Mungo, and Alphie, come with me." They hopped into the back of the Mercedes with practiced ease, and we were off.

Arriving at the church, I parked next to the lay reader, Anne, who was just stepping out of her pale blue Fiat. She smiled warmly and approached as I got out. "Robert, how lovely to see you again. Shall we go inside? Mike the server is already here and—oh gosh, you've brought your dogs! What are their names?"

I introduced the Labs, explaining their hierarchy and hoping they would behave in this new setting. Anne kindly offered to find some water bowls for them, setting a welcoming tone for their church debut.

As the 10:30 AM service approached, everything was in place: the organist played, the choir was robed, and the congregation settled. With children coloring and playing quietly, I offered a prayer in the vestry before checking on the Labs with Anne. They were securely in the vestibule, curiously peeking through the windows at the unfolding service.

As we processed down the aisle, the Labs spotted me and began to vocalize their confusion and desire to join me, their "dad." Their soft moans escalated into a plaintive groan from Alphie, pulling at the heartstrings of anyone who noticed.

Reaching my stall, their voices carried through the church. I addressed the congregation, explaining the situation and apologizing for the disturbance, hoping for a quick settling. That hope was dashed as their moaning continued, unabated by my assurances.

Then, in a moment that felt touched by divine intervention, the churchwarden opened the vestibule doors, allowing the Labs to sit at the back of the church where they could see me clearly. The transformation was immediate: they sat like statues, their eyes fixed on me, their whining ceased. It was as if their only need was to see their "dad" and know everything was alright.

They remained in that spot, silent and attentive, throughout the hour. As the service concluded, I couldn't help but feel a mix of relief and pride. Not only had Millie, Mungo, and Alphie managed to attend their first church service without disrupting it entirely, but they had also shown that with just a bit of visibility, they could be perfect gentlemen.

The congregation's amused and heartwarming reaction as they exited underscored the unique bond between dogs and their owners, and how sometimes, just being seen is enough to calm the most restless spirits.

THE ARTIC FOX LEAP

It was early May, and the garden was a spectacle of blossoms. Almond, cherry, magnolia, and prunus trees sagged under the weight of their floral burdens, their branches bending gracefully toward the earth. The sky was clear, the sun promising a splendid day—perfect for a barbecue in the evening.

"Right, Millie, right, Jasper. How about a walk?" No sooner had the words left my mouth than the two Labradors, previously lounging in their baskets, sprang to life. Tails wagging, eyes bright with anticipation, they were instantly at my side, ready for adventure.

"Let's go around the cross country course," I suggested. "The bluebells are still out, and the bracken seems to shoot up taller by the day. And the brambles—well, they're encroaching on the path more each morning."

We set off, the dogs and I, for a lengthy stroll—I opted for the quad bike, still nursing some pain from a recent hip replacement. We passed the now-empty stables and onto the course. As we approached the first stretch, I paused to admire the winter wheat in the adjacent field. After spending the colder months as mere sprouts, they were now surging skyward, already eighteen inches tall.

Entering the first wood, we hadn't gone far past the beech trees when a pair of rabbits darted from a thicket and disappeared down the hillside. Millie, now an elderly "rabbiter" of nearly

ten years, watched intently. Her hunting days might have been in their twilight, but her spirit was as keen as ever.

Another rabbit sprinted across our path and into a burrow, reigniting Millie's youthful vigor. Moments later, she halted, her nose twitching in the air as she scented another opportunity. With a calculating pause, she then performed a breathtaking leap. Springing from her hind legs, she soared over the ferns in a graceful arc reminiscent of an arctic fox diving through snow—headfirst into the thicket.

There was a brief, pained moan from within, then silence. Millie emerged, backing out triumphantly with a rabbit in her jaws. The chase had ended as quickly as it began, and despite the violent conclusion, there was an air of primal satisfaction—for Millie, at least.

I knew better than to scold her; the rabbit was already beyond saving, and Millie was simply following her instincts. She would carry her prize all the way home, a victorious return from what was possibly one of her last great hunts.

As we made our way back, the peacefulness of the morning resumed. The sun climbed higher, and the promise of the day unfolded before us, marked by the simplicity of life's cycles—growth, chase, capture, and the quiet after.

LYING IN DAD'S ARMS

Millie has the most amazing coat. I am referring to her natural one of course. Thick. Soft. Velvety. Shining. Milk chocolate brown, but with a multitude of other soft browns mixed in. Her eyes were also honeycomb brown, and soft and gently pleading.

Whenever she looked at me, her eyes seemed to always say, 'If I want it, it doesn't matter what it is, if I want anything and I come and stand in front of you, and look at you, and look and look and look. In the end your eyes will meet mine, and then you will give it to me. You can't resist. You know you can't!'

On this evening, supper was over long ago. Both our suppers I mean, and that includes Millie's and Jasper's. Now there was just time for an hour's TV before bed. The four of us head off into the TV room, and after a deal of searching through the TV rubbish, turn onto a wildlife programme. This new programme 'Monkey Business' on Sky Nature will keep us entertained until 1000pm, then we will just watch the BBC news headlines and off to bed.

Whilst we settle down to watch, Millie and Jasper retire to the leather sofa behind me, and with hardly a sound slip on board, one at the left-hand end, the other to the right. They have long ago commandeered it as their own. Gina has, as a matter of precaution and long ago, removed all the cushions.

Ten minutes later, and after a brief nap, Millie slips off the settee and without a sound, processes around to the front of the two of us. We are watching a one-year-old monkey learning from his

mother how to crack open a nut with a stone. Millie sits down in front of me as close as she can get, and then fixes me with both eyes. I try to ignore her. After around two minutes of my not responding, her right paw lands firmly on my knee. I still ignore her.

Millie is never one to be deterred. She edges a little closer and then strikes again, this time with her left paw. When that doesn't work, she moves closer still, and puts her head onto my knee, still gazing intently into my eyes. I look at her briefly again for the seventh time, and quickly look away. I know that if I don't, I am lost.

But I also know, and more important she knows, that my resistance is ebbing away. Eventually she knows that I will say 'Come on then Millie' and as I say it, I stretch out my arms wide. With one bound she is on my lap, then quickly rolling over so that her back is on my tummy, her legs are in the air, and her head on my shoulder.

Within ninety seconds she is fast asleep and she will stay in the same position until the TV is turned off, and we head to bed.

Millie has triumphed. Yet again. She always does!

Millie has the most amazing coat... I am referring to her natural one of course.!. Thick. Soft. Velvety. Shining. Milk chocolate brown, but with a multitude of other soft browns mixed in. Her eyes were also honeycomb brown, and soft and gently pleading.

Whenever she looked at me, her eyes seemed to always say, 'If I want it, it doesn't matter what it is, if I want anything and I come and stand in front of you, and look at you, and look and look and look. In the end your eyes will meet mine, and then you will give it to me. You can't resist. You know you can't!'

On this evening, supper was over long ago. Both our suppers I mean, and that includes Millie's and Jasper's. Now there was just time for an hour's TV before bed. The four of us head off into the TV room, and after a deal of searching through the TV rubbish, turn onto a wildlife programme. This new programme 'Monkey Business' on Sky Nature will keep us entertained until 1000pm, then we will just watch the BBC news headlines and off to bed.

Whilst we settle down to watch, Millie and Jasper retire to the leather sofa behind me, and with hardly a sound slip on board, one at the left-hand end, the other to the right. They have long ago commandeered it as their own. Gina has, as a matter of precaution and long ago, removed all the cushions.

Ten minutes later, and after a brief nap, Millie slips off the settee and without a sound, processes around to the front of the two of us. We are watching a one-year-old monkey learning from his mother how to crack open a nut with a stone. Millie sits down in front of me as close as she can get, and then fixes me with both eyes. I try to ignore her. After around two minutes of my not responding, her right paw lands firmly on my knee. I still ignore her.

Millie is never one to be deterred. She edges a little closer and then strikes again, this time with her left paw. When that doesn't work, she moves closer still, and puts her head onto my knee, still gazing intently into my eyes. I look at her briefly again for the seventh time, and quickly look away. I know that if I don't, I am lost.

But I also know, and more important she knows, that my resistance is ebbing away. Eventually she knows that I will say 'Come on then Millie' and as I say it, I stretch out my arms wide. With one bound she is on my lap, then quickly rolling over so that her back is on my tummy, her legs are in the air, and her head on my shoulder.

Within ninety seconds she is fast asleep and she will stay in the same position until the TV is turned off, and we head to bed.

Millie has triumphed. Yet again. She always does!

LYING WITH MY HEAD ON DAD'S FEET SO THAT I KNOW IF HE MOVES

In Millie's eyes, the world was simple: there was her, and there was her dad, Robert. To her, their bond was unbreakable, a perfect harmony of companionship and mutual adoration. Millie, the chocolate Labrador with eyes as warm as melted caramel, saw Robert as her everything—her protector, her playmate, her world. "He must take me with him everywhere," she'd think, her thoughts as clear as the gentle gaze she fixed upon him daily.

Robert's days were often spent in the solitude of his study, buried in books and papers, while Millie and her brother, Jasper, lounged nearby. Jasper was content to curl up in his favorite armchair, but Millie was ever watchful, her ears perked up at the slightest hint of movement from Robert.

Millie had learned the hard way that naps in her armchair meant waking up to an empty room— the sting of Robert's absence was too much. She needed a fail-safe plan to ensure she would never be left behind again.

Her solution was as clever as it was simple: she would become his shadow, unnoticed but ever-present. The next morning, after a lively walk through the woods—where the wildlife from rabbits to a vocal cock pheasant made their usual appearances—Millie put her plan into action.

As Robert settled into his work, Millie made a subtle but strategic move. She didn't join Jasper in the comfort of the armchair but instead lingered at the study door, her eyes tracking Robert's

every move. Once certain he was engrossed in his tasks, she tiptoed quietly to the other side of his desk.

With a silent grace only a Labrador could manage, Millie laid down directly at Robert's feet, her head gently resting on his shoes. In this position, any attempt to stand up would require him to disturb her, and that slight movement would wake her from even the deepest sleep.

From that day on, Millie's new spot became under the desk, a guardian to Robert's routine. Each time he shifted or even considered getting up, she was instantly alert, her big brown eyes looking up at him as if to say, "Where do you think you're going without me?"

Millie's plan was a resounding success. She had not only found a way to keep from being left behind but had also woven herself even more deeply into the fabric of Robert's daily life. Their bond was stronger for it, a testament to the cleverness and deep love of a devoted dog.

Every movement Robert made was monitored by Millie, and every day ended with the reassurance that she would always be right where she belonged—at his side.

FETCHING A LOG

It is amazing how quickly dogs learn, and how much they seem to understand! Before she was six months old, Millie quickly came to know a whole range of signals from me .... Even though most of the signals that I gave were unintended.

For example, when from time to time I took hold of a box of matches which were kept in the breakfast room, on top of the old kitchen range, her head would come up even if she had been asleep, and she would follow me to the Morning room knowing that I was about to light a log fire.

The first task was to go to the morning room and check the log baskets to make sure that there were enough logs. If the baskets were not full, then I grabbed the baskets and headed down the corridor to the log store situated just outside the back door and which led into the courtyard.

The log store was under cover, and simply two steps from the back door. It made collecting a basketful a very straightforward task.

But Millie was ahead of the game. As soon as the back door was opened, she rushed outside, went to the log store, and grabbed a sizeable log to bring into the fire. Sometimes she decided that two were needed. Once I had filled the basket, we both returned through the back door, and then she led me down the corridor into the morning room.

Once I had lit the fire, and it was ablaze she proceeded to drop her log onto the hearth.

She then headed to the Morning room door, and sat there patiently waiting, as if saying. 'Come on, let's go and get some more!'

THE CAR SEAT WITH HARNESS THEN WITHOUT HARNESS

Come on Millie... in!'

Millie, our chocolate lab, looked towards the opened boot of the Volvo estate car, then turned, and looked towards me, eyes pleading.

You could see in her eyes 'Do I really have to get in?' and then "Well, I suppose if the choice is between staying here just with Mum, or coming with you, wherever you are going, I will get in, because I want to stay with you"

Gosh, how Millie hated the car!

However, with one bound she was in, and she joined Jasper, her twin brother, in the back of the Volvo estate, and we were off.

Every journey had the same preliminaries, which seemed to take forever. She clearly hated car journeys... even short ones.

Because of her phobia I was so very anxious every time we had to make a journey by car. She made it absolutely that clear that she hated being in the boot of the car even when her bed was in there, and she was with Jasper, her twin brother.

What is more there was plenty of room in a very spacious Volvo XC 70, and with windows all round as well. But she clearly felt compromised. On the one hand she was not going to be left behind, but on the other hand she would do anything to avoid a car journey.

When a journey was to be made, the first job was to try to get the luggage into the car without it being seen. This was usually achieved by bringing the luggage downstairs, leaving it in the hallway and then taking the two labs for a short walk whilst the luggage was put aboard onto the back seats.

But the moment she sussed that a car journey was on the agenda, she had a regular routine. She came to the back door to watch the proceedings. She would see Jasper jump in without any concern. Then, following "Come on Millie, into the car", she would turn her head, and remain stubbornly at the door, pretending to neither see nor hear. In the end it was a matter of going back to the door, putting a leash on her, and part dragging, part coaxing, trying to encourage her, and bring her to the rear door of the car and then lift her in.

There had to be a better way surely.

However, a distraction was now ahead of us. Four lovely days by the coast in the North of England It was a great time. Then just under a week later we were back home, having had four days in Northumberland, which, once there, she thoroughly enjoyed. The sea is a magnet for Labradors, and although she didn't swim a lot, she enjoyed paddling, and most of all exploring the sand dunes, and meeting lots of other dogs. On the first evening back at home, we were joined by Nick, our son, with wife Helen and Matthew and Emma their two children. Their car swung into the back drive at around 500pm..I went out to greet them and opened the car passenger front door for Helen to get out. To my astonishment Helen was not there. Instead, there was their Spaniel Mabel neatly curled up on the front seat, wearing a harness, and safely fastened into the car safety strap lockets. 'What is this' I exclaimed, not believing what I was seeing. 'Oh, she wears the harness in the car all the time' Nick responded. 'She adores being on the front seat, and it makes the travelling with her so easy, and she is perfectly safe with her harness oh Now I couldn't believe what I was hearing. A dog safety harness. But yes, it was true. Why hadn't I heard of it before?

Next morning, I was in the car immediately after breakfast and heading for town. The pet shop was my intended destination. Having safely parked the car outside their huge front window, I headed inside, and to my great delight seemed to be the only customer. It took me a long time, but eventually I managed to find a display rack that heralded 'Dog safety harnesses' Upon reading the labels, it was clear that they were intended for car use. Hurrah. But then how many are there? At least eight. Which one do I choose? and they all look so complicated. Better go and find a shop assistant.

Five minutes later the now close at hand shop assistant, had been to the rack with me, and we (him) have selected a harness. So, it is now just a matter of taking it out of the box, and getting a reasonably obedient Millie to stand still for a moment or two (five!) and allow legs and head and tail to be guided into the appropriate apertures. If only it was that simply. Ten minutes later we were not a lot further forward, and a very frustrated assistant suddenly said... 'I think we had better try another one.

The next one seemed easier, and having got Millie into it, I rapidly paid for it, and leaving the harness on her, headed for the car. With one bound she was into the front passenger seat, but it took another five minutes discovering how to attach it to the seat belt locks. However......................

Eventually.........................we headed for home, with a very contented dog lying by my side, with her head on my knee.

Success ....

Two days later, we were making another journey. Out came the harness, and after only three minutes Millie had it firmly attached. I opened the front passenger door of the car, and she clearly knew what was expected, and again with a rapid bound forward she was in. Success? No! Even after ten minutes I could not get the harness locked into the car seat belt locks. I tried first by standing alongside the passenger door, and pushing and pulling the various straps and then, greatly frustrated, jumped into the driver's seat and tried to secure them with me sitting in that position.

Impossible.

Except! Even though not secured to the seat, Millie now had her head again on my knee and seemed completely relaxed. What would happen if I just drove with her like that?? Better do a test. After a few minutes of driving around the internal roads of the estate she had not moved. What was more, it seemed clear that if she could have her head on my knee, she had no wish to move. With a little trepidation I drove the 4 miles to my destination. She never moved, not even an inch and by the time that we got to our destination she was actually asleep.

We had cracked it. For every journey thereafter that was how we travelled. Me in the driver's seat, and Millie in the passenger seat – asleep – but with her head on my knee.

I have no idea what became of the harness!

GETTING LOST

It had been an amazing walk. They always were at Guyzance. The river. The woodland. The arable fields. The meadows that had not changed for a couple of hundred years, and still were ridge and furrow. The wildlife. How it lifts the spirit to be out under the sun (or rain, it doesn't make any difference) in those surroundings.

The river Coquet gurgles its way through the estate for nearly a couple of miles, before then making its way to the coast and allowing its water to join the sea at Warkworth. Sometimes it is gently meandering. In other places it is a rushing whitewater torrent. Here and there it has a huge quantity of enormous boulders breaking the surface of the river and creating foaming bursts of white bubbles rushing through the crevices between them. Once or twice there has been an otter ... or the remains of fish lying on a boulder!

The woodland is set in cascades of trees, some of them tumbling down to the river   With

banks of both deciduous and evergreen trees, and within their depths hiding several groups of Roe deer which make their way down to the water in the gloaming each evening, and again in the early morning to drink.

The arable fields were both my own favourites and the dogs too. The stretches of golden corn... often barley, with a mix of oats and wheat here and there, but with a great number of hares in both Summer and Winter. They are hiding amongst the tall corn in Summer, and the hares

make shallow scoops in the ground in the Winter in which they could lie and do their best to disguise themselves and stay hidden from their enemies.

Moreover, in the banks and hedgerows between the fields, a myriad of wildlife, including rabbits and bank voles. The labs thought that these areas were heaven and would spend a great deal of time meandering up and down both the hedgerows and along the edges of the growing grain trying to disturb and then chase whatever wildlife they could find.

This mid-summer evening walk had been one of the best. We had seen roe deer cross the river. A kingfisher had glided past us as we sat on the riverbank. Millie and Jasper had disturbed three different hares and Jasper had had a chase. He never seemed to learn that he could never beat them for speed! Some pheasants were in the bracken in the set-aside, and after the dogs had flushed them out, they rose with great cackles above the undergrowth, and had then flown to the safety of the woods on the other side of the river.

Now, after a good hour and a half it was time to go home for supper.

But where was Millie.

"Millie. Millie? Come on, come here".

What has happened? She never leaves me. She is never more than a few yards away. What can have happened, where can she be?

I spent the next fifteen minutes driving the quad from field to field, calling, then shouting her name as I went. The into the woodland doing the same thing. Next to the river, driving as close to the bank as I dare. Calling, calling, calling.

Nothing.

I began to feel a little anxious... even scared. Had she chased something into the river, and then gone in herself and become tangled in the branches of a fallen tree. I had heard of dogs doing that and not being able to get free, and eventually drowning. Whatever should I do. I was certain that if all was well with her, she would have come back to me.

An hour later I was quite frightened. Still no sign. Better head for home and leave Jasper there with Gina my wife and then head back to the river and continue the search.

Ten minutes later I raced across the field, and into the drive of West House.

Oh, I don't believe what I am seeing!

Millie got up from the mat by the patio doors, wagged her tail, and came to meet us! I never did discover where she had been.

YOU CHANGED MY COLLAR
FOR DIGGERS!

Digger, Jasper, and Millie were from the same litter.

Digger and Jasper were both boys. And totally black. Millie was a chocolate girl.

Millie and Jasper were ours and lived at the Hall with us. Digger lived with our daughter Alix and her husband Adam.

To find a more laid-back dog than Jasper would be very difficult. Life was fine, if it included breakfast and supper, an occasional walk, and a warm bed to sleep in every night.

Digger, as his name implies was far more animated. Digging holes was a speciality, but on top of that he lived to be active. Long walks, games in the house and garden, there wasn't much time for sleeping (except at night of course). Physically Jasper and Digger were almost identical, and to be sure which was which they wore different colour collars... Jasper, Brown, and Digger red. Jasper and Millie lived with us at Tedsmore Hall, but Digger belonged to our daughter Alix and her husband Adam, and lived at Lodge farm, a half mile away. Alix said that the only way that she tells Digger and Jasper apart, was because Jasper was always so subdued, and Digger so boisterous! She needed the different colour collars to recognize them. Millie was different again from each of the other two. Demure, she clearly knew that she was much more sophisticated than either of the others..and indeed more so than any other dog she met. She clearly showed her disdain for all other dogs given any possible chance. If whilst on a walk a stranger dog came around the corner, her nose went upwards and pointed to the sky. Millie had a fabulous chocolate coat, and with it, unlike most chocolate labs, she had honey-coloured eyes.... It was a fabulous combination. She seemed to know that she was aristocratic.

Despite their very different personalities, they were all very good friends.

One evening in May 2006 Alix and Adam were staying for the weekend, and Gina decided to take them out for supper. I had a load of work to do, and so said that I would stay and get on with my writing but added that I would happily take charge of the dogs.

"Thank you", called Gina, as they left to head away. "We'll be back for around 10:30pm".

The evening quickly flashed by, and as I closed my computer down realized that it was well after 11pm. Not a problem.... I would head to bed and see them all in the morning at breakfast.

Then a thought! Just a thought! It might be a bit of fun and cause a bit of confusion. Why not change the collars of the boys? It might just cause a bit of merriment for a second or two until Alix realized what had happened.

It was done in a trice, and I headed to bed.

Twenty minutes later I didn't hear the door open, as the trio arrived home, and of course as they pushed open the door, they had three dogs welcoming them.

But something was not quite right, Alix knew instantly.

'Digger what is it? Digger what is wrong?' then to the other two, Look   Look at Digger, he's not himself, he must be ill., he has lost his bounce, he is just standing there, and we always get the most enormous welcome.'

In less than ten minutes Alix was completely beside herself. "He must be ill. He must have eaten something. Look, it's obvious that something is totally wrong with him. I need to call the vet and, yes, I know that it is getting on towards midnight, but he might die. I NEED to call the vet".

Then suddenly it dawned on Gina what had happened.

Next morning when I ventured down for breakfast, perhaps you can guess the colour of the air!

THE OTTER AND THE CATCHPOLE DOGS

Today is going to be special, not just two dogs, but five. All of them Labradors. Spending a few days at Guyzance is always a real treat, but when you can be with the Catchpoles from Somerset for a few days and have five Labradors together, that is like being in another world.

Rhona and Graham (Catchpole) live in a delightful hamlet just a few miles outside Taunton called Hele and have a wonderful house – White Stedding – looking South and West, and from where on a good clear day you can see well over twenty miles.

So now at Guyzance together, the morning routine will be much as usual. Up around 8am, take the dogs for just ten minutes into the gardens for a pee, then back for breakfast.

Breakfast is usually over by 9:15ish, and then it's both of us men onto the quad bike and head off through the estate and down towards the river. After around half a mile, one can join the river loop (as we call it) and follows the river Coquet for almost two miles, and then end up going under a viaduct where the East Coast Main railway line crosses the Guyzance estate. From there we usually leave the pasture, and head through three of four fields of wheat and barley, and into some woodland. In the woods you can do a circuit, emerging at a different point to the point of entry, and then follow a similar route home. On almost every walk, one can see roe deer, hares, rabbits, pheasants, buzzards, heron, ducks, geese, and often a lot more wildlife than I have described here. Magic. An hour of pure magic. The dogs of course just love every moment.

They chase the deer, the hares, the rabbits, and anything else that moves. And amusing but true, they never catch anything. The chase usually lasts only a few minutes, and the dogs return exhausted.

This day was pale grey sky but still with warmth from the hidden sun. We had gone under the viaduct and then through the woodland, it now was time to head for home for a coffee.

As we emerged from the wheatfield, and then through the gate back into pasture just 100 yards from the viaduct to our amazement, a black figure bobbed into view in the middle of the field, some fifty yards from the Coquet.

The dogs saw it instantly and raced away and towards it.

An otter. A dog otter. My God he was huge, and spotting the dogs rapidly bearing down on him, he headed towards the river as fast as he could in that magnificent lolloping gait.

The otter just about reached the water first and vanished with an enormous splash. Within a second or two five Labradors followed, and moments later six heads were bobbing around in the middle of the river. The labs saw him and swam as fast as they could towards the otter. The otter vanished into the depths, and then to our amazement suddenly with a single bounce leapt out onto the bank, but with the dogs still in the water and frantically searching everywhere with their eyes. The moment they saw that he had emerged from the river, they themselves headed for the bank.

Within a couple of seconds five dogs were also scrambling onto the bank, intent on bearing down on their quarry. But by now the otter was nowhere to be seen. As they had come out of the water, the otter had launched himself from the bank and back into the deepest part of the river.

What perfect timing!

He was never seen again!

WELL, IF NO-ONE WANTS THAT SALMON I'LL HAVE IT

Graham had always loved fishing. So, he and Rhona had come to join us in Northumberland for a few days, and during the daytime Graham was hoping to fish the river Coquet   Weather and water permitting.!

The first day that we were there was clear, warm, and sunny, and to recall the words of John Cannon the Ghillie, perhaps a little too bright for the fish.

Nevertheless, being down by the water is always a special experience. Today was no exception. BY 900am we were on the bank, rods primed with bait, clear water gently gliding past us, and looking forward to our first fish. It was not to be, not even a nibble, and by twelve forty-five we were back home having a simple lunch of bread and cheese with a little of the green stuff which I dislike intensely and am certain was only edible by rabbits.

I always try to ignore it, but somehow it seems to find its way onto my plate, and I have no choice.

An hour later we were back at the river. Once again with the sand, the stones, the pebbles, and the rocks at the bottom of the river glistening in the current, and as always it was a joy to be there. From nowhere two Roe deer emerged from the wooded slopes on the opposite side, stood for a few seconds on the other bank, then saw us, tossed their heads, and vanished back into the trees.

Moments later a kingfisher raced past us downstream, low to the water, and with a flash of red, blue, and green. The next two hours seemed to race past, and suddenly John reminded us that we had wives back at the hall, and we had promised that we would be home by 5:00pm and join them for a cup of tea.

There had not been a fish in sight all day.

The next morning dawned with a totally clear sky, and the sun beating down relentlessly. Even at nine o'clock the temperature had reached 22 degrees Celsius. Then the silence was broken by the sound of a quad bike coming up the drive and parking outside as John Cannon arrived to escort us for our days fishing. John didn't drive, but he had a lovely Honda quad which he used for all his journeys to and from the hall. We went outside to join him. "Are you sure that you want to go today?" John asked meekly. "It's going to be sunny and hot all day. Not the kind of weather that the fish like. They will probably lie low close to the bank and be totally uninterested in anything that we throw out towards them in the water".

Before I could speak, Graham had made his own thoughts very clear. "I have come 300 hundred miles to fish for a couple of days", he said, "and what is more I just love being by the water and in the water. Nothing on God's earth would stop me fishing, so just hang on five minutes John and we will be with you".

Six minutes later after I had collected my own quad from the garage, two quad bikes roared into life, but this time with two of us on board mine, we all headed down to the river. 'I think that we will fish down on woodside' John said. 'The river runs between two extensive banks of beech and ash trees there, and there might be a bit of shade, and it will give us a better chance of making a catch.'

Once the quads were parked up in the shade of a large beech, we set to work. Within minutes three rods had had flies attached and were being guided along the surface of the river. Graham and I were close to each other, but John had donned his waders and   and then clambered into the river, and within a few minutes was forty yards downstream, and casting into one of the named pools which he knew that the salmon commonly frequented.

Today we had brought lunch with us, because the ladies had decided to go first to Bambrough castle, and from there on to Craster to try to buy some kippers and possibly some lobsters and slip into the Jolly Fisherman for a one course lunch.

Just as it was coming towards twelve thirty, we could see John making his way upstream and heading back towards us. 'Time for lunch' he called, 'I'll get it ready for you' At that precise moment there was the very recognisable whirl of a fishing line being run out at high speed , and Graham shouted T think I've got a bite' I watched the ripple on the surface of the water run upstream past us, and then within seconds come back downstream like a streak of lightning, To my amazement and my delight, this time for just a moment I could see the fish. It looked to be a good size salmon. Graham played' the fish up and down the current for a good three minutes, but eventually managed to bring it close to the bank, and then with John's help, got it into his keep net. It was brought onto the bank, the hook disengaged from its mouth, and with a very quick movement of his hammer (the 'Priest' he called it) John gave it the last rites, and it lay motionless in Grahams arms.

"It's around fifteen pounds' John said, "quite a catch. Well done".

Graham was thrilled.

90

We had a very quick lunch, and it was obvious that Graham was keen to get back to the water's edge with his rod and line.

We were just putting the remains of the picnic into the hamper, when to our surprise our two wives arrived. 'The Jolly fisherman was fully booked' Rhona said, and so we have slipped back home to collect the dogs, and now come to join you to share your sandwiches and your wine.'

As the five Labradors bounced around us, it was at that moment Rhona saw the fish. 'Gosh Graham, well done let me get my camera. Pick it up and hold your fish in front of you I need to capture this moment for the children to see' Graham stood proudly with John Cannon at his side and numerous images were recorded. Photography finished Graham lay his fish onto the grass and began to prepare for the afternoon session. John and I did the same, and the two women sat down on the bank to enjoy the river and the sunshine.

Suddenly the silence was broken by John Cannon exclaiming "Good heavens... look at that... Jasper stop......................Jasper drop it   . Jasper no".

Jasper our black lab, was advancing towards us with Graham's fifteen-pound salmon firmly clenched between his teeth. I could have sworn that he was smiling, and his smile was saying 'Look what I have found. This wonderful salmon was just lying on the grass. No-one wanted it. So, I've decided that it is mine'.

When eventually he obeyed the shouts and laid the salmon down onto the grass there wasn't a tooth mark to be seen anywhere on the skin.

what amazingly soft mouths Labradors have.

EYEBALL TO EYEBALL

Millie the chocolate Labrador was lying on the rug in the main sitting room, looking at me with pleading eyes.

We had already done a five-mile quad bike walk down to the railway viaduct and the woods beyond. We of course being me on the quad, Millie, and her twin brother Jasper. But of course, five miles to a Labrador is a mere trifle. She would happily do ten, I knew that, and given half a chance she would probably keep on going for the entire day.

I tried to ignore her and concentrate on the SODUKO that I was attempting. The daily Telegraph 'Diabolical' which came out each Friday was always a challenge, and I always tried to find half an hour to attempt it.

Quite suddenly I realised that there was a wet nose on my knee. I looked down, and the pleading eyes of Millie looked straight into mine. Jasper was out for the count. Not that he wouldn't wake instantly if a walk was offered, I knew that.

Graham had gone with John down to the river again to try their luck. Yesterday's catch of the salmon had been a moment to savour for Graham, and he was sure that there were more large fish simply waiting him. They had been gone for a good hour. 'I wonder if they have had a bite' I mused. 'Perhaps we should go to find out'.

Millie's eyes were still pleading, and the rug around me was a little wet with dribble. 'Okay' I murmured 'Is anyone coming for a walk?' Like a flash both dogs were at my knees, with eyes twinkling brightly. Knowing that to reach the fishermen I would have to go for a half mile on the road, and therefore the quad would not be appropriate transport, I grabbed the keys to the Volvo, and headed for the door. Within seconds we were heading towards the road, with two dogs in the back clearly anxious to get to somewhere they could have a good run.

I stopped at the gate to the monastery field, slipped out and opened it, and then drove down the side of river to the far end where I knew that the two of them would probably be.

I was right. Just past the burial ground I espied them both on the bank, rods in hand, so I braked the car to a halt, pressed the boot key to let both dogs out, and then jumped out to join the two men, and see what ....if anything..they had caught.

Suddenly, and without warning, Millie was in the river. She loved the water, and hardly ever resisted the chance for a swim, 'if that dog stays in the water, we haven't a chance of seeing any fish for the next several hours' John warned.

I should have known better than to let her out of the Volvo, but the deed was done, then only thing now was to get her out of the river, and back into the car. 'Millie... come out' I pleaded. 'Millie, out... out', but to no avail. Indeed, the opposite seemed to be happening, as she turned her nose towards the opposite bank and headed towards the middle of the river.

Then the impossible happened. We couldn't believe our little eyes. A salmon surfaced alongside Millie and for at least two seconds they swam eyeball to eyeball along the surface of the water. You could almost see each of them 'start' with surprise at finding themselves alongside another creature. Moreover, even though their heads were alongside each other, the tail of the salmon could be seen behind the dog's rump. It was a big fish indeed, at least three feet in Length. And then she was gone. The salmon, of course, not Millie.

I turned to look at John Cannon.

Was he angry?

Would he have a go at me for allowing my dog out of the car?

What was he thinking?

"I've been fishing for fifty years", he said "Never seen nothing like this. If only I had had my camera, because no-one is ever going to believe me when I tell em what I have seen today".

THE ARRIVAL OF ALPHIE

We were sitting having a simple lunch. Me a cup o' soup, and a mousse, Gina a little cheese, and the usual piece of fruit... today an apple. I said quietly 'Millie and Jasper are getting old. They are coming towards the end of their lives. Are we going to have some more when the time comes?' Gina turned and looked at me. "Well,", she said, "That is a big decision. You are 71. If we had a puppy now, it may well live twelve years. You will then be 83 or 84. Will you - will we - be able to cope with the walks and the feeding and all that goes with looking after a dog at that age? If we wait until these two are no longer with us, that could be another 3 or 4 years. And so, with the same scenario you could be 88!"

"What are you saying?" I asked.

There was a long silence and then, "I think that I am saying that if we are going to do it, we ought to do it now".

So, the decision was made, and we discovered that a business colleague of ours in the Northeast had a litter of puppies almost ready to go to new homes.

Ten days later, Gina set off with the grandsons, Charlie, and Bertie, to help make the final choice once they could see the puppies. They also needed to gauge whether they were suitable and would mix well with the two back home, and if so, which one to choose.

Eight hours later they were back at Tedsmore, with dog basket in the boot, and with a new puppy inside. Gina had telephoned me from the car to tell me that the trip had been successful, and the new pup was male, black, and named Alphie!

Millie and Jasper of course heard the car coming up the long drive and rushed out to through the back door, barking and jumping to see who it might be. As the Volvo came through the archway, and then stopped in the Courtyard near to the back door, both Millie and Jasper heard the engine turned off, and rushed towards the car to greet their mum, tails wagging. They knew that she had been away quite a long time, she might have been shopping and might have brought a treat back with her, even perhaps a delicious bone for each of them.

Gina smiled, and then called the two dogs to her. I stood by the door watching. 'Millie, Jasper, I have a lovely surprise for you.............and for daddy .... come and see' She opened the car boot, lifted out the dog basket, and opened the lid. Alphie, a tiny black bundle was quickly carefully lifted out, and put down to the ground. He sprang high into the air as puppies do, making quite an entrance. Then he stood motionless, looking around at his new surroundings, taking everything in, and assuming the air of the new kid on the block. An air of being completely king of all he surveyed.

Millie was rooted to the spot. You could see in her eyes she was thinking 'Why? ', 'What is this' 'What have they done'. Then she looked first at me, then looked at Gina, and walked past the puppy head held high into the air.

It was as if she was saying, 'I am queen here, and I didn't want any courtiers.'

'She didn't go near Alphie for nine days. Clearly it was going to take a little time for the new occupant to be accepted. If ever!

Of course, he was accepted, and after around two weeks, they became good friends).

WHAT'S THE VET BILL FOR?

"Robert, I have just got back from the vets".

I looked at the clock above the kitchen door and saw that it was just past six o'clock. Great, the sun is over the yardarm. That can only mean one thing.

"Fine Gina, would you care for a glass of wine before supper?"

'Yes please. But whilst I was there David (the vet) asked me to pay the bill for your visit last week. So, I did!'

I handed her a glass of Sancerre, and then took a sip from my own.

'Right' I said 'That's great. Shall I make a few canapes to go with the Sancerre. I saw a few prawns in the fridge left over from last night.'

'That would be lovely, but first tell me about your visit to the vets last week   why did you take Alphie to see him at his surgery?'

'Didn't David tell you?'

'Yes, but I want to hear it from you, I want you to tell me exactly what happened.'

Oh, it was nothing, I just decided to take him for a very quick check.'

'Why did he need a check…. And why didn't you tell me?'

'Truly it was nothing of any consequence, it wasn't even worth mentioning to you.'

'David told me that you ran over him on the quad bike.'

Time to beat a hasty retreat. And perhaps time to change vets. Why can't people keep their mouths closed. Is nothing private anymore. The dog is still alive, surely that is the main thing.

'Well, 'I said 'It happened like this, T took out the three of them, Millie, Jasper, and Alphie (who was still only ten weeks old), went through the wood, and when we came to the studded gate at the back of the walled garden realized that I would have to reverse a couple of yards. So, I glanced around and all three of them were five or six yards away exploring under the chestnut trees, whereupon I threw the quad into reverse gear to spin round.

What I hadn't seen, was that during that brief, instant, Alphie, had left the other two and was now sniffing under the quad bike, and as I reversed, I just caught his tail.

He yelped a little, and although he seemed fine and I couldn't find any injury of any sort, I thought that he should just be checked by the vet.

'Lucky that was all. He's a lucky boy. It could have been much worse. You should have told me'.

And there the conversation ended. Gosh, off the hook again.

Factually, as I reversed the quad there was the most earsplitting howl. I hit the brake instantly, and there was little Alphie, with a part of his appendage under the rear wheel. Knowing there was no-one around, I clearly had to deal with the problem myself.

The best way, I was sure, was to throw the machine into forward gear, and drive forward to release the tail. As I edged forward there was another howl, and as I looked down, I saw that Alphie had not been released. I edged forward again, sure that this time he would be free. Another air splitting howl. I looked down again. It must be that the quad was dragging him along by the tail as it moved forward.

Nothing else for it. Jump off the quad, and with a great effort try to lift the backend of the vehicle. At the third attempt I succeeded to get it around seven inches off the ground. But it was enough. Alphie was free, and he then raced around though the wood, in and out of shrubs and ferns as if there was no tomorrow.

He was fine. And me? I was off the hook yet again.

(Footnote from Gina: His tail is bent!)

THE ARRIVAL OF MUNGO

"Millie and Jasper are both getting old. They are showing their years. At almost eleven years, they may not be with us that much longer".

Gina put down her planting trowel, looked very pensive for a moment, and then added 'Not many Labradors get beyond twelve. We need to prepare ourselves that the end is coming. It will be a big blow emotionally.'

"Yes, it will be a big shock when the day comes, I know that. We both love them both dearly, and they obviously can't be replaced. Nevertheless, I am keen that we go on having a couple of dogs, and yes, we now have had Alphie for a couple of years, but I am keen to have a pair. It may well mean that we are going to have four for a short time, but, let me ring Harry in Durham and see Tony Trimble on Tees-side and see if he has any lab pups on the way"

The phone call was made and with a positive outcome.

Once again, a few weeks later Gina was in her car heading to the NE to collect Mungo. She had already been up to the home of Tony on the Moors just South of Darlington with her grandsons, and they had inspected the litter and chosen Alphie, a very active black boy Labrador, and brought him back to Tedsmore. Now that Mungo was just a little over eight weeks old, he could also now be collected and brought back to Shropshire and join us.

Round about four in the afternoon, I had taken Millie and Jasper with Alphie for their usual afternoon walk. Two to three miles. Me on the Honda quad bike, the three of them walking and running alongside, but stopping every few yards to explore all the smells on route, and with Alphie trying to find any stick worthy of the name, and that might be worth taking home and adding to his growing pile.

As we returned through the arches garden towards the house, I realized that Gina's Volvo was coming up the drive towards the house.

Excellent, I thought. Time for these three dogs to be introduced to the newcomer. I drove the quad through the tall stone seventeenth century Archway into the Courtyard and turned off the engine. Gina had already parked and was busy extracting a dog carrier from the boot of the estate car.

"Who is this?" I turned towards Millie and Jasper. "You have a new brother joining us here at Tedsmore. Come and see. It is very exciting".

Gina dropped the door of the dog carrier, and Mungo tumbled out and into the Tedsmore world. As he saw the other three dogs, he stopped short, his hackles immediately raised.

Jasper seemed pleased, and he advanced on the youngster. Millie's reaction was totally different. Just as she had done with Alphie, she looked aghast (if a dog can look aghast), and she turned bn her heel' (on her back legs) tossed her head high into the air and walked away from Mungo towards the house. She made it abundantly clear that she couldn't understand why we had done it. 'You have me — why could you possibly need another dog, and that makes it four. And what's more, yet again it is a dog and not another female.... I must just have forgiven that.' It was very clear that as far as Millie he, the new black boy, was not at all welcome.

To my great surprise, Mungo turned towards Alphie and quickly went over to him, and then rubbed noses, and smelt Alphie's undercarriage. It was if he was saying 'I know that you are my brother! (they had then same mother) Moreover, Mungo made it quite clear from that very moment that he was number one—he was superior to his older brother. Nevertheless, they became good friends quickly, even though Alphie remained a little cautious whenever his brother approached him.

For the next three weeks Millie again ignored the newly acquired puppy completely. He clearly wanted to make acquaintance with her and try to be friends but Millie was having none of it. Every time he approached her, her nose went high into the air, and she headed off in the other direction. Once or twice, there was even a very low growl, making it quite clear that she wanted to have nothing to do with him.

It was around a month later, when she was heading from her bed to the kitchen for breakfast, that Mungo came round the corner of the corridor from the courtyard garden where he had been out to do his morning ablutions and walked straight into her.

'Gosh' I anguished. 'Is there going to be showdown?'

But by that simple encounter the ice was broken, and from that moment it was as if Millie had said 'Oh well, in a few month's time you will be as big as me, and furthermore you are a male, a lot younger, and probably will want to rule the roost.'

But in fact, Millie remained 'in charge' right to the very end of her life!

BITING ALPHIE'S SCROTUM

Mungo had just arrived.

Now ten weeks old, and a bundle of animated fun

He was a very handsome black boy.

A Labrador of course.

A magnificent, shaped head with fabulous large flowing ears and a cowlick down the centre of his nose. Two very large appealing eyes, dark brown towards black in colour.

But within hours it was clear that he was a bit of a bully.

Not toward Millie and Jasper, who of course were ten years older than he, but it seemed that his half-brother was fair game.

Whenever Alphie (the half-brother) had something that he felt he should possess, he was determined to get it, and get it he usually did. His normal method was to grab hold of whatever he wanted and pull and pull, and sometimes even gently growl to make the point. In most cases Alphie eventually let go of the said object, whereupon Mungo retreated triumphantly with the trophy in his mouth.

Then suddenly, without any warning whatsoever his tactic changed.

I was bringing the four of them into towards the house after a lengthy quad bike ride. We had had a lot of fun. Millie had almost caught a rabbit, but after a chase through a thicket had narrowly missed it and given up. Jasper had found a sizeable puddle, and because of his love for water, had jumped in headfirst, but then had restrained himself a little bit, and only spent three of four minutes splashing around.

Alphie had had a few sticks thrown for him at different points along the walk and had raced after them and rescued them from wherever they had fallen, then to find that Mungo had wrestled them from him, carried them for twenty yards, only to then drop them once again. Once they had been dropped, and Mungo showed no further interest in the sticks, Alphie was able to quietly retrieve them, and carry them towards home.

The usual practice though was that once we were within twenty yards of the house Mungo again went to Alphie and wrestled and wrestled with him, until he was able to take the stick (s) from him that he, Alphie, was carrying, somehow it seemed of great importance to him that he actually carried these sticks over the threshold and into the house.

But today something amazing happened, and I was totally taken aback at the developments.

Alphie was by now only stone's throw from the backdoor, and still triumphantly bearing his very large stick. Very quietly Mungo sidled up to him, came alongside so that the backs of the two dogs were side by side, and then reached down and quite clearly bit Alphies scrotum. There was a yelp, the stick was dropped, and Mungo headed towards the door with his trophy in his mouth.

Had I really seen what I had seen? Could it really be the case that Mungo knew that by biting Alphie's scrotal sack, he would quickly be given whatever Alphie was carrying. Surely, I must have mistaken what I had seen, or thought that I had seen.?

The next day brought an absolute repeat of the episode. It was quite clear. Mungo was deliberately biting Alphie in the (now missing) balls to get him to drop what he was carrying, so that he, Mungo, could have it.

Amazing.

Then it happened again the next day.

And the next.

But the following day, Alphie was ahead of the game. As we approached the door to the house, and Mungo began his move, Alphie dropped his sticks and headed away at speed. He wasn't going to be taken for a mug for a fourth time! Mungo picked up the sticks in triumph... that was his intention all along, but Alphie had escaped the mauling.

Thereafter every day was a repeat, and Alphie did not have to experience any further traumas of being bitten on his undercarriage.

What two very bright dogs!

....it was almost unbelievable!

THE RYTON XI TOWN VET

I have been sitting on the lawn mower for three hours. It is a beautiful Saturday afternoon. Now it is coming up towards 430pm. It has been sunny for the whole time that I have been grass cutting. It has been a perfect day to have spent as many hours in the garden as one can spare. Now it would be good to have a cup of tea, so turn the ride-on lawn mower homewards, and head back to the house.

As I reach the back door, Gina, my wife is just coming out, her car keys in her left hand.

I'm going to fetch Jasper from David's at Ryton' she told me. 'Really, I didn't know he was going to the vets' I replied 'Is he all right.? What has happened?'

Gina stopped, turned round, and followed me back into the house. 'Well,' she said, 'I have just had a phone call from the Vets. The receptionist told me that a couple with a Volvo estate has just turned up there, with Jasper in the back of the car. She told me that Jasper led them into the surgery, and as they went through the door, the receptionist said, "Oh hello Jasper, why are you here?"

Then apparently, she said to the couple 'That is Jasper Parker, one of the Labradors from Tedsmore hall. We know him well, why have brought him in to us?' The lady replied 'Oh we don't know the area very well. We are just having a pleasant day out in the country. As we drove past these rather imposing gates leading up to a big house, this black lab was outside the gates, quite close to the road, and we thought that he looked rather lost. So, we put him in the back of our car, asked the next person that we saw where the nearest vets was, and here we are'

The receptionist said rather acidly, 'As I told you, that is Jasper, and that is where he lives. He was at home before you collected him! If you leave him with us, I will call the owner, and I am sure that either Robert or Gina will come and fetch him.'

Having finished telling me her story, Gina left to continue her rescue mission.

Half an hour later Jasper's adventure was over, and he was back home.

You could almost see the twinkle in his eye!

I'LL JUMP OFF THE QUAD TO CATCH THAT RABBIT

Jasper was coming up to his eleventh birthday. It was clear that all was not well. His energy had gone. His enthusiasm seemed to have drained away. His appetite was minimal. He had better be taken to see his friend David.!

David, the family vet, was inspirational. Always gentle and kind. Always understanding. Always prepared to put himself out and make time available, even out of hours. Even though he sometimes did things which the dogs found difficult, like sticking needles through their skin, they seemed to trust him, and Millie and Jasper had no problem in going into the vet's surgery, and then into the consulting room.

By ten thirty next morning we had made the three-mile journey to Ryton and were in the waiting room. Jasper as usual seemed to be totally unconcerned about the other three dogs there, even though the Alsatian was making it clear that he didn't like Jasper. Thank goodness the Alsatian was wearing a muzzle.

Twenty minutes later the consulting room door was flung wide open, and David came through. 'Jasper' he said,' Your turn, come on in.'

I put my magazine away, got up and followed David back into the consulting room, with Jasper following on his leash.

'On the table, please,' said David. Jasper was no lightweight, but after the second attempt he was now standing on the table. For the next ten minutes David gave him a good examination. 'If you can leave him for the morning, I'd like to X-ray him. If we give you a call after lunch, can you come and pick him up them?' 'Yes of course', and so we headed for home.

At three twenty the telephone rang, and a voice said, 'Hi, this Amanda at Green Hollow vets, Jasper is ready to come home. Oh, and when you arrive, please don't go without having a word with David.'

Twenty minutes later we were face to face with David. 'Not good news' he began 'I am pretty sure that it is cancer of the spleen, I can operate, but there is no guarantee of success, and at his age! '

'What do you recommend David' 'I think it is probably best if he comes with you and lives out his life with TLC. It isn't going to be very long mind you.'

Decision made!

Next morning, I went to find Steve the gardener. 'Steve, can you make me a cradle for the front of the quad bike please? Jasper has cancer and is not going to recover. He isn't walking very far, but if there is a cradle he can come with me alongside the quad for his walk, and when he gets tired, I can lift him into the cradle.'

A couple of hours later the cradle was made, secured to the front panier of the Quad, and filled with blankets.

Robert, Millie, and Jasper set off for a delayed morning walk Fifteen minutes into the walk, and quite close to the reservoir in the wood, Jasper came to a halt. Clearly, he had enough and wasn't going to make it home. Two minutes later we were on the way threading our way on the uphill track between the beech trees, but now Jasper had been lifted in, and was sitting in the cradle. Alert. Content. Ears pricked. Watching intently on all sides for any interesting movements such as a rabbit......................(that was Jasper)

Immensely surprised (that was me!)

As we left the woodland track, to our left there was a thicket of bramble, bracken, and coppiced beech. Suddenly a large rabbit shot out from the thicket and across the track. Millie was nowhere to be seen. In a trice, Jasper was up, and launched himself, and was in rapid pursuit of the quarry. Rabbit escaped with ease. Jasper returned very quickly but was clearly exhausted. It took me a huge effort to get him back into the pannier. If I possibly, could I needed to make sure that that didn't happen again.

Thereafter twice a day Jasper went for his morning and evening walk in the pannier on the quad. Even though his strength was failing, he clearly loved it. Sometimes lying down, sometimes sitting bolt upright, he never tired of this rather unique journey. For the next ten days, even as his energy levels were diminishing to almost nothing, he clearly enjoyed his new routine   his exercise.'

Sadly, it was to come an end all too quickly.

THE LAST QUAD BIKE RIDE

Seven fifteen. The alarm has just sounded. Another day just starting. By the look of it, with the sun streaming through the trees, another glorious day. Need to get downstairs and see how Jasper is. He seemed even more frail and weak last night at bedtime. It was an effort for him to go outside and walk across to the flower bed and have a 'pee'. He had to be really coaxed to get up and come to the door in the hall.

Downstairs. 'Jasper, where are you?' He normally comes to the kitchen door with Millie to greet me as I come down. But not today. Millie is there but no sign of her twin. 'Jasper. Jasper?

Oh, there you are, why are you are still in your bed. Come on... come on outside?

Jasper, come on. Jasper please. Come outside for a pee.'

No movement whatsoever from the bed. He didn't seem to be in distress but hadn't the energy to try. What to do. Better call David I think, he will give the best advice.

Just ten minutes to midday, and David was with us, and Jasper had had a full examination. 'Sorry Gina, sorry Robert, nothing I can do. I think the end has come, you need to make the decision, but if you want to me to, I have the injection in my car. Shall I fetch it?'

'David, please can we delay till after lunch. I'd like to give him one last quad bike walk in the panier' "If I come back at 2:30pm?' 'That will be fine. Let's say 2:30pm.'

Copa soup and yoghurt later, and it was one forty-five. Steve the gardener had been alerted earlier and he was knocking at the kitchen door. He carried Jasper outside and placed him in the panier. Immediately Jasper sat up and looked round. I was on the quad with engine purring, and Millie had joined us. We set off to do the twenty minutes around the cross-country course. Jasper sat up all the way round, and more than once seemed to want to launch himself after two squirrels and a rabbit that dared to cross our path. He hadn't the energy and so with ears still pricked stayed in the panier and just watched them.

By 2:30pm we were back at the house.

David was waiting in the courtyard garden. 'Don't lift him down' he said, 'he can stay on the quad.'

I cradled his head in my arms, and he nuzzled into me. I looked away as David readied himself for the injection. A minute later the breathing had stopped, and Jasper was completely lifeless. I flung myself off the quad, rushed to other side of the garden, and the tears flowed uncontrollably.

A comforting arm appeared from nowhere around my shoulder, and Gina said, 'Steve has prepared everything, let's go with Steve and bury him now.'

I drove the quad out of the courtyard, and into the beautiful woodland at the back of the house. Steve had dug a grave, and within seconds Jasper had been lifted gently down, placed into the grave, and was buried.

A wonderful life... that had given us so much joy,   had come to an end.

114

GUYZANCE AND THE WEDDING DRESS

Guyzance is in Northumberland. A beautiful tiny village set only five miles from the coast, where the North Sea rolls in and out of some of the most exquisite sandy coves and bays in England.

August the eleventh dawned another blue-sky day. Cloudless. The trees softly murmured in the gentlest breeze imaginable. The air was pure and clear, and looking out from the house across the lawn towards the West one could see for twenty miles. After I had had breakfast, I sat near the patio glass doors and watched a couple of magpies quarter the grass, taking insects as they went. As I watched them a couple of Roe deer emerged from the shadows of the beech trees fringing the lawn, and cautiously edged across the rolling meadow towards the gulley on the Western side, munching the sweet grass as they went.

Suddenly they froze. Then I realized that Alphie the youngest of our three labs had put his nose out of the open patio door ....and he had been instantly spotted.

In a trice the Roe were away, and in no more than fifteen bounds had covered the forty plus meters to the edge of the lawn, and then vanished into the gulley. Alphie had watched them as if mesmerized. At only six months old, he was still a playful puppy, and although now almost full grown a potential chase was often of no interest. Although he had seemed quite captivated by the deer, he had made no attempt to follow them as they raced away.

In a way I shouldn't have been too surprised. I had taken Millie, Jasper, and Alphie for their morning walk some three hours earlier, and having gone around the river loop, we had come to our favourite sandy beach on one of the languid bends of the river Coquet.

Alphie loved that beach. Even when we were still one hundred yards away, he headed off towards it, and then waited patiently at the top of the riverbank for me to arrive. Millie at ten years old still paddled regularly and occasionally swam, but her twin Jasper was content to stay in the shallows.

But not Alphie, he adored being in the water.

Once I had jumped off the quad, and grabbed a couple of sticks, Alphie, as always, barked and barked. He knew what was coming.

Whilst Millie and Jasper explored the undergrowth, Alphie and I went down to the edge of the river water, and I threw his stick for him ten or twelve times. At this point the river is around twenty meters across, and the stick skimmed over the surface of the water, stopping very near to the opposite bank. Alphie was in his absolute element, and within seconds had retrieved it and brought it back to me.

The previous night had seen quite a lot of rain, so in addition to the paths being slippery and very wet, the river was quite high. After a five-mile walk, and ten vigorous swims, he was quite a tired boy!

At around 1pm I decided that the day was so glorious that I would like to go down to the river again. 'Come on, you three' I called, and they were with me at once. I mounted the trusty old quad, pressed the starter button and we were away. Over the meadow, past the sheep, and into the Hall gardens. I suddenly realized that we had agreed to a wedding being staged at the hall that weekend, and quite a few of the wedding guests were out on the main terrace and lawn, sipping a glass of something bubbly, and enjoying the warm sunshine before the ceremony began.

I waved and hurtled past them.

Ten minutes later we were again at the sandy beach, and again I was watching Alphie retrieve his stick from the waters of the Coquet. Millie and Mungo had vanished, but I knew that I only had to call them, and they would re-appear at once.

My tenth throw of the stick found it enmeshed in a willow sapling growing horizontally out of the opposite bank and very low across the water. After six attempts it was still firmly wedged. Alphie had failed to retrieve it, and I decided that no matter how many attempts he had he wouldn't dislodge it. It was a bit of a struggle to persuade him to give it up, but eventually that was accomplished.

Time to go home!

Back onto the saddle of the quad, and with three dogs in tow, we head through the barley stubble, and back towards the Hall.

As we emerged from the lower wood and came onto the lawn just below the walled garden where the wedding ceremony was taking place, it suddenly occurred to me that I had forgotten all about the wedding. Gosh, we might be about to disturb the most important and sacred part of the ceremony. But there was no need to worry. The ceremony was long completed, and bride was now dangled on the arm of her newly acquired husband sipping a glass of champagne. She looked beautiful in a full length white gown and had a sparkling diamante tiara in her hair. Guests were all around her, all with glasses in their hands. It was a beautiful sight with the rolling manicured lawns, a magnificent eighteenth castellated building as a backdrop, and a blue sky above.

Then I reeled with horror. Alphie, wet with mud and river water, was racing at full speed through the gates to the lawn and then rushing towards the guests. I tried to open my mouth to call him, but no sound came out. Within less than a second, he had bounded up to the bride and groom, and then with great glee bounced off the grass, landing with his chin very close to hers. When he had descended from her bosom back onto the grass, the bride was an amazing sight. From her chin to her ankles, she was a mixture of gooey brown, black, green, and white. Except for her face which was whiter than snow. And the expression on it was very difficult to describe. Every guest had frozen. I sat, mouth open, completely motionless on the quad, wondering what kind of bill for compensation might be about to be sent to me.

Then to my amazement her father rescued me. He guffawed with laughter. 'Well darling' he shouted, 'You have said every day for a year that you want a unique wedding. Well, you have certainly had one. No other bride has ever looked quite like that.'

And in an instant every guest burst into laughter, and then they were quickly followed by the bride. A potentially disastrous situation had been totally dissolved by the bride's father's comment.

I didn't say a word, but made a very hasty retreat, and to my surprise found that I had three very obedient dogs in tow.

MATCHES FORA BBQ

It was a glorious July day. The morning had dawned without a cloud in the sky, and the 'blue yonder' stayed that way right through the afternoon and evening. What is more there was hardly any wind. Just a faint rustle of leaves as the boughs of the trees rocked gently to and for. It was now 730pm. Time to light the BBQ, I decided.

Gina had got some sausage and a couple of steaks out of the freezer, and had also prepared some sweet corn, mushrooms, and peppers. White wine was chilling, and the red wine in the decanter was being allowed to breathe a little air, so that it could reach room temperature before being served and had therefore been placed just to the left-hand side of the warming plate on the Aga.

I look down at three sleeping Labradors! What a pity it would be to disturb them! 'BBQ' I intoned gently. Three sleeping dogs woke up instantly. As they bounded up to me together it was difficult to believe that a few moments earlier they had been fast asleep (apparently) and now looked as if they were joined by an umbilical cord, tails wagging. When I took hold of the box of matches from the dresser, and shook it, and repeated the words 'BBQ' the tempo of the tail wag increased manyfold, and Millie jumped up to try to take hold of the box of matches. 'Whose coming for a BBQ?' I asked, but without any need to do so. Millie, Alphie, and Mungo were already heading towards the kitchen door that leads through the Hall, into the Morning room and then out to the garden, ...to the croquet lawn where the BBQ lives, together with a large rectangular table and eight chairs.

I followed them matches in hand, and then watched as at high speed they all bounded through the hall, into the morning room, where Alphie and Millie both made a detour via the log basket which was near the fireplace.

Each of them bent over the log basket and emerged triumphantly with a thin log. They then each looked me in the eye. It was as if they were saying 'You can't have a BBQ without logs, and we know that we have to do our bit if we are to each be given a sausage at the end of supper

....and sometimes when we are very helpful.

We even get two ....and it might be today! '

And when Mum is away, it has even been known on the odd occasion, for dad to give us each three!

TAKING THE RABBIT OFF MUNGO AND SHOWING HIM HOW TO DEAL WITH IT

It was his first birthday for Mungo, one of the black labs. We had come up to Guyzance in Northumberland for a few days in the middle of March. All three dogs loved being there. Millie the chocolate girl, and Alphie, half-brother of Mungo and the same colour as him, being another black boy. Out from the house each morning at 7, into the estate woodland and then round the river loop. We usually managed a good two-mile trip with me on the quad bike leading them. They had their favourite spots on the walk of course. Halfway round the loop there is a sandy shingly beach that runs for around 100 yards alongside the river. Millie, now 11, had given up swimming, but often had a paddle. Mungo swam a little bit; bit was always cautious about going more than elbow deep. Alphie was a male mermaid. He absolutely loved the water, and carried a stick for the last half mile before we got to the water so that he could be sure that there was a stick to be thrown for him. The Coquet (the name of the river) is around 30 yards wide at that point, and on the occasions that I managed a good throw I could land the stick in the water, close to the opposite bank. Alphie always swam out with great gusto, grabbed the stick, and swam back with it in his mouth onto the shingle, dropped it at my feet, and barked until it was thrown for him again.

We had done all that. Alphie was exhausted, and now we were on our home.

As we approached the top field, a young rabbit shot out of the hedge, with Mungo in hot pursuit. Mungo had never caught a rabbit. Was this to be a first? To my amazement he caught up with it and pounced. He managed to secure the rabbit in his mouth and carried it about 5 yards before he dropped it. To Mungo's surprise it ran away. Mungo chased it, caught it again, and again dropped it. The poor thing ran for another four or five yards. Alphie was oblivious and was only interested in the stick that he had carried from the river. Millie was twenty yards away, and because she was intent on investigating a rabbit hole in the bank, hadn't seen what was happening. Mungo dropped the rabbit for a third time, and again it ran. 'Come on Mungo' I thought 'Surely it is intuitive for a dog to know what to do with a rabbit once it has caught it' Yet again Mungo gave chase. Suddenly Millie looked up from the bank by the hedge and saw the rabbit. She covered the twenty yards in under three seconds, and as soon as she was there alongside her stepbrother chasing fleeing rabbit, she pounced, and 'bang' it was all over. The rabbit's life had ended.

Mungo clearly watched the entire episode with great interest.

You could almost see him thinking 'So that's how you do it. Lesson learned.'

Now Mungo is four. …….. and he still has never killed a rabbit. Come to think about it, that is the only one that he has ever caught!

The lesson was clearly not very well learnt.

MILLIE IS ILL

It is sixteen months since Jasper died, this morning Millie seems to be off colour. I do hope that nothing is wrong.

During these past sixteen months, she has seemed to be in great shape. Chasing balls, climbing onto my knee as I watch TV. Lying on my feet as I work at my desk. Eating her meals without any holding back or seeming lack of appetite. Going for thrice daily walks, and still wanting more.

Even so, she does seem to not be herself, better call David again, he will call in and just make sure that all is well.

Later that afternoon David arrived at the house, and Millie was given a thorough examination. 'Can't be sure' David said 'but after the way that you have described her, and then a full examination, I am afraid that she may have pancreatic cancer. But   we needn't give up just yet. There's quite a lot that we can do, and she may well have a reasonable life quality for some months.

My heart sank. Then, after he had given her a couple of injections, and as David pulled away in his car, I decided that I had to face reality, and even if Millie had a terminal condition, I needed to make her last few weeks, or months, as good as possible.

Furthermore, if she was going to become frailer, and have less energy, the first thing to do was to call Steve and have put the basket back onto the Quad bike panier and fill it full of blankets.

That way she could still have her three times a day walk, but just like her brother, they could be in the basket.

Only twenty-four hours later and she seemed to have worsened. It was six o'clock, and time for the evening walk. Gina was away in Devon, so I decided that we would have our walk and follow it with a BBQ.

For the first time my beautiful chocolate Lab seemed reluctant to go out. I picked her up and gently put her into the basket on the quad. Thank goodness. Her demeanor changed instantly. She was alert. Head turning this way and that. Clearly, she was keen to go.

Forty minutes later we were back. 'BBQ, BBQ' and Millie was all attention. Four of us Robert, Millie, Mungo, and Alphie munched our way through a pound of sausage, four beefburgers, and some loin of pork. I also had some barbequed mushrooms and a couple of sweet corn cobs. Delicious.

'Right' I said 'Let's find a pudding' and headed into the kitchen to explore the fridge. After a deal of rummaging, I discovered the remains of a bread-and-butter pudding, and some yoghurts. I remembered that Nick, eldest son, had been with us a couple of days earlier, and this was the leftovers from his visit. The Bread-and-butter pudding was only four days old, must still be alright... especially if it was given a quick burst in the microwave.

Once outside I decided to play safe and shared the bread-and-butter pudding three ways, and then I settled down with a raspberry yoghurt. The pudding was soon gone. I glanced at my watch and realized that it was almost nine o'clock and was beginning to go dark.

Millie was lying down at the side of my chair, when, to my surprise, she got up, and headed through the arch and out of the courtyard. 'Good girl, Millie' I called after her. She had clearly gone to do her nights oblations and would be back in a few moments.

Two minutes. Nothing.

Five minutes. Nothing. I was concerned.

Ten minutes. Still nothing. I was alarmed.

I walked swiftly to the archway at the front of the courtyard and called into the garden. 'Millie, Millie. Come here... where are you?'

Silence. Nothing. I was very worried.

Millie had vanished.

STEVE TO THE RESCUE

My Millie had been gone now for twenty minutes. It had never happened before. Wherever I went, she came too. But tonight she had completely vanished.

But not to worry. She will soon come back to the sound of the Quad bike engine. She always comes to the sound of the quad. So, I dashed round behind the house to the garage, jump swiftly up onto the saddle, and turn the key. The 2hp engine roared into life, and we (the quad and I) were away. Into the gardens, calling at every tree and bush. 'Millie. Millie... come here.'

Nothing.

Through the arches garden, round into the arboretum, and then a U-turn, and head back to go along the woodland between the house and road.

'Millie... come here... please ....now. Millie'

After ten minutes there was still no sign. Clearly, I needed help. Better go and call Steve the gardener. Back to the house, grab the phone. 'Steve, please I need help Millie has disappeared. Totally vanished. I've been looking for her for at least fifteen minutes.

'Don't worry was the reply. 'I'll be with you in ten.'

Eight minutes later, the smiling 6' 4" tall Steve — thin as a rake — came into the courtyard, closely followed by Tracey, his lovely, voluptuous wife. I quickly explained what had happened.

'We had a BBQ followed by puddings. She suddenly got up and went out of the Courtyard. I was sure that she had gone to do her ablutions. But she didn't come back. Where on earth can she be?'

All three of us headed back into the gardens, calling as we went.

As we reached a rhododendron thicket, Steve stopped, and said very softly 'She's under there. 'Millie come out. Millie. Millie.' There was neither a sound nor a movement.

Clearly Steve was wrong, perhaps there had been a rabbit. In a trice Steve lay down on the grass and crawled under the Rhoda. Within a few moments, he was coming out again, but now feet first, Millie firmly between his arms. I was amazed. What on earth was going on?

Back at the house, we put her onto her bed. Outside it was growing dark. 'Don't let her out again commanded Steve. 'No, I'll make sure that she stays with me' I replied.

I sat alongside Millie's bed for around fifteen minutes. Outside the night had grown darker, and there were beautiful traces of orange and red in the sky to the West. Without warning Millie stood up and headed for the back door. She stood there silently, eyes pleading. 'She definitely wants to go out and do a pee' I said to myself. 'She never stands by the door except when her bladder is full.'

'Millie, come on back inside the house and onto your bed' I pleaded, but move she did not.

I turned the doorknob and opened the door. In an instant she was gone. 'Just into the Courtyard' I told myself, 'She will be back in a moment'.

How wrong can you be! Ten minutes later, and after calling frantically once again, I was again on the phone to Steve! 'Steve terribly sorry, but she has gone again.'

There was a silence.

Then 'I'll just change out of my jim-jams, and I' be with you '

And again, after around ten minutes, Steve and Tracey were at the door.

I explained what had, happened, and apologized profusely. 'Sorry, I should have kept her in, but she seemed so determined to go out, and I was sure it was just for a pee!'!

We headed down to the same Rhoda bush She was bound to be there of course. But this time the cupboard was bare. Twenty minutes later, and after a huge amount of searching, there was still no sign. Steve had been checking all the bushes that we came to ... I had no idea that there were so many in the gardens. Then calling all the way, we headed back to courtyard by the house. Steve went straight to a magnificent 'Bride' bush just be the gate. It must have been eight feet tall, twenty feet wide, and stretched right down to the ground.

'She's there' Steve mumbled. I bent down and looked intensely into the darkness, but I saw nothing at all. Once again Steve lay down on the ground and crawled into the depths of the bush...................................'No Steve, if that is where she wants to be, let's leave her until morning.'

'We can't do that, badgers will find her and kill her' And once again he crawled into the inner depths of the shrub, and he emerged with Millie in his arms. Thankfully I took her from him and headed back into the house.

I put Millie into her bed and sat with her until 100am She seemed fine. Her eyes bright. Looking at me intently from time to time. Finally, tiredness got the better of me and after giving her a hug, and saying goodnight, I headed upstairs.

Next morning, I was and dressed by seven. Straight down the stairs, opening the door to the kitchen and called for her, and at same time thinking. 'How Strange... there was no sign she was always waiting at the door to greet me.'

Then To her room, and gosh, she wasn't in her bed, and so back to the kitchen.

Then I saw her. Prostrate. Lying by the door to the garden.

She had deadly breathed her last and had been dead for some hours. Then it dawned on me. She had known. She had known that death was very close. When she had headed away the previous evening, it wasn't for a pee at all. She had gone to find a cool dark place on the bare earth, and spend her last solitary moments there, quietly by herself.

I had deprived her of her final wish!

Now she and Jasper lie together in the old Victorian pet cemetery in the woods. Their grave is surrounded by wrought iron railings reminding one of Highgate cemetery in London.

Nothing is too good for that wonderful pair.

Nothing.

TIME FOR A BBQ

Mungo has one main concern in life. His tummy!

Wherever he is, whatever he is doing, at the first sign of food, he instantly loses interest in whatever he has been engaged in and focuses on the meal or snack that might be just around the corner. It was quite hard still to believe that at a very early age, he learned that when I grabbed a box of matches, it meant that a BBQ was probably just a few moments away.

The preparations for a BBQ in our house follow a standard routine. Get a couple of trays and put them onto the central island in the kitchen. Mungo sits up and takes note, and watches carefully what might happen next.

Load the first tray with plates, cutlery, wine glasses, salts, and peppers. Mungo becomes even more alert.

Then the second tray is got ready with the basting oil and brush, the salad stuff, and any vegetables that might be going to be included in the cooking of the meal, such as mushrooms and peppers and sweet corn kernels, and then finally the meat. Sausage, chicken thighs, steaks, lamb, or pork filet slices come out of the fridge and onto the tray, etc.

When these last begin to appear, Mungo finds it very hard to contain himself, and simply must come forward to the edge of the island, and put himself on sentry duty, and especially to guard the tray with the meat on it.

Then comes the coup d'état. I shout BBQ, grab the matches, and toss them towards Mungo, who catches them and instantly heads towards the door that leads to the walled garden.

BBQ time is very close!

THE CANDLE AT NIGHT

My Millie has been gone (died!) for a month tomorrow. I miss her so much. When I come downstairs each morning,

I stupidly look to see if she is on her bed. When we are in the garden, and I hear dogs running towards me (Alphie and Mungo) I look up expecting her to be with them. When I come in late at night after a long day away, and the dogs rush to the door to greet me, I expect her to be one of them welcoming me.

And so tomorrow is going to be a very tough day. What can

I do soften the emotions and the pain.

It is coming towards 1030pm. Time to take Mungo and Alphie for their final walk of the day usually just twenty minutes around the garden and through the woods. As I pick up my headlight from my desk, and prepare to put it on, I suddenly see a birthday candle flare in a box just to the side of my desk. An idea comes immediately. I grab the candle flare, and head towards the kitchen to find some matches. I find some at the side of the Aga, and pocket them, and head towards the door, to go to the garage for the quad bike. Both dogs are at my side,   as always.

The quad engine fires up, and she roars into action. We head through the courtyard, and I take an immediate left turn, past the bowling green folly, and into the arboretum. Then across the lawn, past the bamboo, and within ninety seconds I am alongside the graves of Millie and Jasper.

This little burial ground also contains the final remains of Felix, the tomcat who we inherited on arrival at Tedsmore, and two other dogs, long deceased before we arrived, and each having a very fine headstone made of local stone and each around two feet tall.

I turned off the quad engine, and immediately the two labs sat down and turned to look at me. It was as if they were saying 'What the hell are you doing in the middle of the night? This is a very strange place to bring us '

I took the birthday-flare from my jacket pocket and pushed it into the soft earth at the foot of Millie's grave. There then followed quite a lengthy search for the matches. Eventually I found them tucked inside my shirt pocket. There was a light breeze and since I did not bother to guard the flame, the first match went out quickly, and then the second did the same. But the third held on gallantly, long enough for me to reach down and touch the white substance within the top of the flare. The candle sprang into immediate life, and the night sky blazed with light. All three of us sat there silently watching the spectacle.

'Thank you, Millie, for sharing a wonderful life ' I said, and then as an important afterthought 'Thank you Jasper.'

The candle blazed for around 30 seconds. It was a beautiful experience and seemed to bring my very special girl Millie very close.

From then on, on the fourth of every month, the three of us took a candle flare, and sat mesmerized, watching it light up the trees all around us, and for a few moments bringing Millie back to life.

... at least that was how it seemed!

IF YOU EAT IT, IT MUST BE GOOD.

Tonight, it is not my favourite.

Gina seems to manage to weave a salad into the supper meal rotation about once or twice a week. Yes, they are okay, but rabbits eat salad stuff, not human beings. To be fair she does try to make it interesting, but in my humble view, that is not possible. Gina will minimize the lettuce and the tomatoes, and include things like avocados, sweet corn (on the cob) peppers, and radishes. She calls it a crunchy salad,.

She normally gives me a warning. She appears at my study door, about an hour before the meal, and says something like 'it is a salad tonight, is that all right?' I'm not quite sure what would happen if I were to say 'no'. But of course, I never do that. I simply raise my eyebrows, and mutter, 'yes of course'

Tonight, I am heading into the TV room, tray in hand (well, in both hands actually) and being led by Mungo who as always will be hoping for a scrap at the end of my meal.

I always tell him that it is a salad, and that he needs to temper his hopes with reality. Nevertheless, he leads me into the TV room as usual, and once I am in my favorite chair, as always, he sits around a meter away from me and eyeballs me.

Tonight, besides all the green stuff, there are a couple of slices of ham, and an avocado filled with prawns, and on the side of the plate just a little smoked salmon. Quite a feast and probably more than enough protein to help wash down the green stuff. However, when I had finished what I would describe as the main content of the meal, there was still quite a lot left on the plate, including some carrot sticks, a couple of radishes, and few tufts of lettuce.

Mungo had sat at my side throughout, watching each mouthful intently. So, why not?

let's try him with a carrot stick first. I know that when there are carrots with a main course like a casserole, that has some delicious gravy, if I dip a carrot in the gravy, he will wolf it down. So, what will he do with a bare unadulterated carrot?

Gosh, it has gone ....without even a pause for breath.

So, let's try a radish. Gosh that has gone down as well   without even bothering to smell it. Okay, a couple more carrot sticks and another radish, then we will need to prepare for the ultimate... the piece of lettuce.

Okay, so all the carrot pieces and the radishes have gone... instantly   but surely lettuce will be different altogether.

So, pick up the lettuce and offer it! Mungo carefully smells it, and then draws back and looks at me. Next, he looks me straight in the eye as if to say 'What is this? it's green. It has no smell. It has no substance. You can't be serious in expecting me to eat it?'

And then it was gone.

He looked me in the eye again, and this time was clearly saying 'Well, I saw you eat some of it. I'm not sure why you did, but you did. So, it must be food of some sort. So, I have eaten it as well. I hope you now feel satisfied!'

I CAUGHT A RABBIT!

It is astonishing how dogs can be so different.

Millie seemed to be on a mission to catch rabbits all her life, and regularly succeeded with her arctic fox leap (see story on page 41)

Jasper was equally enthusiastic, but caught very few, and clearly had no thoughts about emulating his sister, and using the artic fox leap technique.

But even though they watched Millie on a regular basis, neither Mungo nor Alphie seemed really interested. Least of all Alphie, for whom the only thing in life that seemed to be worth chasing, was either a ball or a stick. From time to time, when Mungo came across a rabbit he might give a halfhearted chase for about ten yards, but never broke into a sweat, and never got anywhere near it.

Millie & Jasper & Digger

Today we are staying at Guyzance hall for a few days, and so there will be some very extensive walks by the river, which both dogs love.

Then out of the blue, as we turned the corner out of the wood, around twenty yards ahead of us, Mungo spied a large rabbit sitting on the path and it seemed to be quite oblivious to our presence.

Instantly Mungo's ears went to 'alert', and for the first time in his life he went into stalking mode. He crept up on unsuspecting rabbit and managed to get to within two yards of it. There was still no obvious recognition by the poor creature that his life might be in imminent danger.

Mungo pounced and there was a yelp from the rabbit. There was huge gasp which came out of my mouth. Had Mungo, after all the failed attempts, finally caught his first rabbit. But it was clear that he had the rabbit gripped firmly in his mouth and held in a squeeze around the animal's midriff.

The rabbits head lolled onto one side. The animal was dead.

Mungo came back towards me. I was sure that he had a smile on his face. The poor thing was dropped at my feet, and I bent down and picked it up, much more in sadness than in triumph. Yes, I know that a dog's instinct is to kill   but I hate the ending of any creature's life we all, every single living thing, have a right to life, and no-one should kill another creature... animal, bird. insect, fish etc. unless there is the need to eat it for food, or one's life is in danger.

I rolled the rabbit in my hands and turned its face towards me. I should have known or course I should have known.

Eyes closed and hugely enlarged. A lot of infected tissue on the head around the eyes and nose.

The rabbit was completely blind. The rabbit had myxomatosis.

It was hardly a moment of great triumph for Mungo. He had killed a rabbit that was near to death and could probably neither see nor hear anything!

A STICK!

Between the Hall and the rear Courtyard where the ride-on lawn mowers and the quad are kept, and there is also the log store, there is a narrow-covered passageway. Probably around a meter in width. In that same passageway there are kept quite a few containers, one for plastic waste, one for cardboard and so on... there to keep them dry. It also means that we can take out bits of waste from the kitchen and reach these bins without getting soaked if it is raining cats and dogs!

When I bring the dogs back from their walk it is the shortest and quickest route back into the house.

Problem!

Yes, today there is a real problem.

Alphie usually arrives home with sticks, carries them as far as the garage and then waits with them in his mouth until I have parked the quad, but is still determined to take them through the passageway as far as the back door.

A few days ago, he managed to carry back from his walk a stick at least 80cm long, and probably weighing a kilogram. He was holding it well off centre, probably one third, two thirds. When we got to the passageway, the left-hand end of his stick immediately banged into the corner stone of the passageway. I guess that it might well have been painful. To my total surprise Alphie then backed away a little, dropped the stick, and proceeded to pick it up again, but this time holding

it exactly in the centre. Problem solved, and he carried it through the passage without either end hitting the wall.

Today we have a real problem. He has brought back the biggest stick you have ever seen. At least one hundred and thirty centimetres long, and there is no way he can get it through the passageway. I know that, just be looking at it, and he is about to find out!

I park the quad, and call to them, 'Come on boys, time for breakfast' and I head for the passageway followed by them both, and with Alphie leading. 'Rang crash both ends of his stick, collide with the stonework. He backs off, drops the stick, and then picks it up again, holding it dead centre. He then tries again. "Thud, smash, wallop' there is no doubt that he is beaten.

But Alphie is never beaten.

Again, he backed away, and then simply turned and went the long way round the drive, totally avoiding the passageway and simply met me at the back door.

Since then, he seems to just know the length of the stick that he has found to bring home.

Either the stick will go through, and in which case if he needs to do so, he has learnt to drop it, and pick it up at the centre, and carry it through the passage to the back door where he drops it. (he is not allowed to bring it into the house, pain of death... that is pain of my death, not his) ....

Or he knows that its won't go through the passage, and so he doesn't even try. He just goes round the other way and meets me when I emerge from the passage! How brilliant is that.! A dog with an IQ of 120?

IT'S PUDDING TIME

It is so lovely having a wife who can cook.

I wish that I had one.

Sorry, I got that wrong, of course I do!

Supper times at Tedsmore have always followed a formula. I am usually at my desk working, and round about 7:00pm I can always hear the sounds in the kitchen of a meal being prepared. At around 7:30pm the timer begins to sound three of four times. On the third or fourth occasion it is immediately followed by the shout, 'Robert, Dinner is ready'. Unless I have my computer turned off within five seconds, and am on the way to the kitchen, there is always a second far more strident shout.

Two trays are prepared; knives and forks, spoons, salt and pepper, and there are often two glasses on the worktop, one of which is empty, and the other with the remnants of a drink poured round about half an hour before. I usually then fill both glasses, getting them ready to accompany the meal.

Once the meal has been plated, they are carried through to the TV room, and we are always accompanied by the dogs.

Gina and I settle into our two armchairs and try to find a TV programme that we feel is worth watching. Alphie settles himself on the leather sofa, whilst Jasper comes and sits in front of me and eyeballs me for the next ten minutes whilst I eat the main course to our meal. He sometimes gets a little treat, and sometimes Alphie deigns to get of the sofa and come and have a treat.

At this point both dogs retreat to the comfort of the leather sofa.

Usually, we then watch the TV programme for the next half hour, until there is either a change of programme, or a break in the ads.

Gina then usually says 'Are you going to do puddings?' Puddings! It is a magic word. In one bound Mungo is off the sofa, and standing in front me, tail wagging vigorously, looking me straight in the eyes. As I stand up, he immediately goes to the TV room door stands there waiting, wagging his tail, ready to go back to the kitchen.

He knows that whatever the pudding, Gina will almost certainly have SKYA yoghurt on it. She will scoop it out of the pot on to her dessert bowl with a large dessert spoon.

Mungo will always get to lick the spoon.

'Pudding' is an important word if you are a black Labrador.

THE ARROW SPIKES

Every day was either a "chase the ball day" or a "bat and ball day."

Alphie knew it, and I knew it. Sometimes six off the roof, but...

Every day around 1:30 pm, Alphie would pick up a ball from somewhere, bring it to me at my desk, drop it at my feet, and then just sit. If I ignored him long enough, he might then give a gentle growl. There was no choice. Put on a hat and coat, find the homemade bat in the porch, and head into the arboretum. Alphie danced along all the way, the tennis ball in his mouth.

Once we were clear of the house and through the archway and onto the grass, we always followed the same routine. Alphie danced up to me, dropped the ball at my feet, and barked vigorously! I stooped to pick up the ball, and then whacked it as hard as I could across the lawned arboretum, usually managing to get it about fifty yards away. Even before I had hit it, Alphie had gone like a rocket. He seemed to know exactly the trajectory and direction that the ball would take, and at times was even there before it hit the ground, and as it came down, he often managed to catch it.

Then it was simply a matter of pick it up, whack it again, and then continue the process. Through the arboretum, across the arches garden, into the large Victorian walled garden, back into the main lawned area, and then head for home. He usually managed to have around twenty chases, spread over half an hour. At the end of this he was exhausted but still ready for more.

This sunny day, we had just left the Victorian walled garden, and I had gathered the ball and gave it a massive swipe towards one of the flower beds at the far end, probably forty yards distance. Alphie was as always gone like a bullet from a rifle.

All the Tedsmore flower beds are edged with cast iron spiked railings about a foot high to keep the rabbits out. As soon as the ball dropped into the bed, Alphie launched himself into the flower bed to retrieve it. Unfortunately, the beddings and shrubs had grown high enough to completely hide the railings, and Alphie didn't see them and had forgotten that they were there. There was a loud high-pitched yelp!

I was extremely alarmed and wondered whether he might be badly injured. Then to my relief, he raced to my side, dropped the ball, and barked as usual. I swiped the ball away again with the bat.

Again, he was gone and within a moment was back, dropping the ball at my feet and barking madly.

A couple more swipes of the ball, and a couple more retrieves, and we were at the back door. Bat and ball game over for another day.

I opened the door, and we both went inside. Having put my coat away, I headed for my study.

Horror of horrors. There was blood everywhere.

I called Alphie to me, and he was leaching blood from his stomach like a leaking pipe. Ten minutes later we were at the vets. David was horrified. "Best leave him," he said. "I will operate straight away

---

(Footnote from Gina: The wound was deep and jagged, and needed extensive embroidery. It was three weeks before all the stitches could be removed. Now Alphie is very wary of collecting any ball that lands in the undergrowth. Lesson learnt.)

THE RACE HOME

Alphie loves to run and now he has found a new game.

Twice each day, we go for our quad bike walk. I do about 2 miles, and Mungo and Alphie probably about five! It's quite intriguing that Alphie has his own paths that he enjoys and those that he avoids.

The woodland that we drive through is a myriad of interlaced pathways, and Mungo sticks like glue to the route chosen for the quad. He is never more than ten yards away from me, wherever I go. Whichever route I take, he waits at each intersection to see which way I am going to turn, and then bounds off in front of me, often narrowly missing my front off-side.

Alphie, on the other hand, has a very different agenda. He is always intent on doing his own thing and very often disappears down a track that I only use occasionally, only to reappear at an intersection further on. Then he stands there waiting for me, almost looking as if he is laughing at me and saying, "Where the hell have you been?"

But then when we get back to the house, he has discovered a brand-new game. As we emerge through the gate from the Equestrian center into the Arches Garden, I throw the quad up through the gears and hit the accelerator. He also hits his own accelerator, and the race is on towards the house, probably a quarter of a mile distant.

We use totally different routes. I use the driveway, and Alphie always chooses the shortest distance, across the lawns, and then through the Arboretum.

And no matter how fast I go—and it is very easy on the quad to reach up to 40 km per hour—but no matter what speed I do, when I get to the beautiful sandstone arch that leads into the inner courtyard of the house, where the back door is located... he is always there waiting for me. Always, never out of breath, a glint in his eye, tail wagging, motionless, and as if he is saying, "What kept you?"

SIX OFF THE ROOF

Alphie was completely ball and stick mad. Whenever I (or anyone else) picked up a ball or a stick, he danced with expectation. And he danced and danced and danced—like a kangaroo.

"Can we do six?" I would say to him, and he danced more excitedly, his teeth flashing as he sprang up from the ground in anticipation. You might have thought that he was smiling.

Into the backyard, and round to the log store, which had a shallow angled roof, and with the lowest part only around 2 meters from the ground. Alphie danced some more, and this time couldn't contain his excitement, and the dancing he soon accompanied with some sweet high-pitched music (high-pitched barks!). It was as if he was playing a complete range of classical brass and woodwind instruments.

"One," I cried, tossing the ball into the air, and up and away onto the roof. Alphie's eyes never left the ball's trajectory for a second, and after one bounce on the roof, and as it flew in the open space around us, he leapt into the air and caught it cleanly. In less than a second, it had been dropped at my feet.

"Two," I called gently, and again tossed the ball upwards and this time a little higher. Two bounces on the roof, and again as he danced the highland fling in readiness, his eyes never left the tennis ball. As it curved down towards the ground, he flung his body upwards and caught it still 2 meters from the ground.

"Three" and then "four" followed in broadly the same pattern, and with the same result.

"Now!" I cried, "High five… are you ready?" Alphie was clearly ready. What a stupid question. His high-pitched moans filled the air, and he bounced continually waiting for the moment. I flung the ball upwards as hard as I could manage. Again, it curved through the air, and landed on the highest part of the log store roof. Three bounces later, it was still traveling at high speed as it hurtled towards the ground. Did that matter? Not a jot. Alphie flung himself upwards and had the ball in his mouth in a trice. And then again, amidst all the moans, it was dropped at my feet within a moment.

"Last one, six," I told him sternly, and the ball was up and away for the last time. It was caught with great ease as it came off the roof, but this time was brought to me and dropped at my feet with a real lament, which went on and on. It sounded like an operatic ballad from a tragedy. "Please dad, more, more, more!"

And when I picked up the ball and headed towards the house door, the opera continued all the way into the house.

"Six? Only six?" "Oh, come on dad, it should be six hundred!"

THE RAILWAY ROOM

I've had a secret vice; one I can admit to. Since the age of minus six (that's where I started at birth; my wife says I'm now two and a half), I've been fascinated by trains. As a boy, I'd spend hours by a railway line, just 100 yards from our house, watching them go by—express passenger trains, local passengers, freight trains, coal trains. They were all fascinating. Gradually, I found that it wasn't just the locomotives, magnificent though they were, that held my interest. It was the logistics surrounding the railway. Where do trains come from? Where are they going? Why? What are they doing? If they are freights, what cargo are they carrying? Who works out the timetable? Who enables the massive number of trains to get through a junction like Rugby and do so in an orderly fashion so that every train stays on time? (or not!)

Out of this fascination grew a longing to have a model railway. The first one was built by me (with a little help from my father!) at the age of ten (me, not my dad!). It was built on a sheet of board measuring eight feet by four feet. And it was brilliant, with three engines, two stations, and four sidings for freight. I spent hours running trains round and round and round. Mind you, it was difficult to include any meaningful timetable for a railway of that size.

That was more than sixty-five years ago! Now, six layouts later, things have moved on. The current model railway occupies a room that is one hundred and six feet long and forty feet wide. The gauge has changed from being 1:76 scale to 1:43 scale. Everything is almost eight times as big as it was sixty years ago. A locomotive is eighteen inches long and weighs ten to fifteen pounds. Every train has a purpose. The timetable is, like the real railway, for seven days. It takes the

operators six months to get through a week, and when they have done so, every train is then back where it started the timetable week.

Moreover, this latest railway has attracted quite a following. Every Thursday around nine in the morning, retired men (most like me, aged two and a half) start arriving. They leave about ten p.m. in the evening. Altogether about thirty men come to the railway. They all contribute in so many ways: carpenters, electricians, loco repairers, scenery builders, track cleaners, carriage and wagon builders. The contributions are endless and invaluable. Usually, on an average day, maybe fifteen or so, and sometimes quite a lot more, turn up.

Around one o'clock, we stop for lunch. Sandwiches, hot noodles, soup, pork pies, cake, crisps, and much more find its way onto the lunchtime menu.

Is it strange then, that when I am at home on a Thursday morning, just after nine o'clock, if I say 'does anybody want to be a railway dog', I instantly have four volunteers with constantly wagging tails? Furthermore, I scarcely have time to open the car boot before four dogs are inside and clearly desperate to go with me to the railway. They know that it will soon be lunchtime, and all four of them have learned very quickly what that means.

It's great having around fifteen grown men join you for lunch.

Especially when every one of them is a sucker for Labradors!

TROTTING UP THE DRIVE

It had been a long drive all the way down from Northumberland to Shropshire, but at last, we were nearly home.

It's amazing how the dogs always seem to sense that the journey is almost over; no doubt, they are greatly looking forward to stretching their legs. They sleep in the back of the Mercedes for much of the journey, but over the last mile, just three minutes from home, they stand up and begin to look out of the car windows. I often wonder if there are smells that signal to them, "nearly home!"

The first time I made this journey with them in the back, and we came through the Estate gates onto the drive, I stopped the car and remotely opened the tailgate. The Labradors were out in a flash—Mungo to the left, onto the grass to have a pee against one of the trees, and to smell who else had been around in his absence. Alphie, on the other hand, went straight to the right and into the woodland to do his business in private.

I then put the car into automatic and headed towards the back door and the courtyard, anxious to also get to the loo and have a cup of tea. As soon as I did so, it was clear that the dogs disapproved because they were anxious not to get left behind. They chased me all the way up the drive and then followed me into the courtyard at top speed.

Ever since that first journey, the routine has changed. Now, as soon as I release the tailgate, they jump out but immediately rush to the front door of the car. Then, at a very sedate pace, they

lead me all the way up the drive to the courtyard and the house door. They occasionally still stop for a pee, but when they do, one of them remains on the drive to prevent me from getting past them. They have no intention of either being left behind again or being made to dash up the drive as fast as their legs can carry them in case I decide to head off somewhere without them.

This same procedure has been followed every time we arrive home after a journey. I was never again allowed to go ahead of them up the drive ever again. I might just disappear.

(Footnote from Gina: If only!)

TOM'S RAILWAY ARRIVAL

Tom, at 94, stood as a testament to a life well-lived. A former policeman who had traded his badge for retirement nearly four decades ago, he carried his age with the grace of someone who had found contentment in quieter pursuits. His slim frame and the slight curve of his spine did little to slow him down, especially with Netta, his lifelong partner, by his side. Together, they navigated the golden years with resilience and a shared love for life's simpler joys.

In retirement, Tom had discovered a passion for railways that mirrored the dedication of his younger years on the force. His particular interest lay in the world of model railways, a hobby that brought him to my O gauge railway setup housed in a spacious, air-conditioned building not far from my main residence. It was more than a hobby; it was a gathering place, a community hub where about 25 fellow enthusiasts convened every Thursday to share in the meticulous care and expansion of this miniature world.

The Labradors, Mungo and Alphie, had become as much a part of these Thursday gatherings as any human participant. They spent the day in peaceful repose, curled up on a rolled-up carpet beneath the sprawling setup, emerging with clockwork precision at coffee and lunchtimes to mingle and partake in the day's offerings. These moments were as eagerly anticipated by the dogs as they were by the group, a testament to the bonds formed not just between people, but between people and their pets.

But the highlight of every Thursday, the moment that seemed to elevate the day from merely special to truly anticipated, was Tom's arrival. The dogs sensed his approach even before the sound of his car engine reached the rest of us, their excitement a clear signal of his imminent entrance. Their barking was a fanfare announcing not just the arrival of a beloved friend but of a moment they treasured above all others.

As I opened the shed door to let the eager Labradors out, the scene that unfolded was one of pure joy. Tom, with Mungo and Alphie in tow, would make his grand entrance, pockets laden with treats courtesy of Netta's thoughtful preparation. It was a ritual that spoke volumes of the care and affection that permeated not just their marriage but extended to their four-legged friends.

Mungo and Alphie, ever the opportunists, wasted no time ensuring that Tom's generosity was well exploited—though always with an unspoken agreement of fairness between the two. Yet, in Mungo's eyes, there lurked a playful ambition, a hint of a plan forming to one day claim all the treats for himself. It was a light-hearted aspiration, one that added an extra layer of amusement to our Thursday rituals.

These gatherings, marked by laughter, shared interests, and the simple joy of companionship, underscored the beauty of community and the unique ways in which our lives intertwine. Tom, with his gentle presence and pocketful of doggie treats, embodied the spirit of generosity and connection that made every Thursday a day to remember.